Stranded in Space

Bob Doerr

The Enchanted Coin Series

Book 4

A Mouse Gate™ Adventure

Mouse Gate Press
1103 Middlecreek
Friendswood, Texas 77546
281-992-3131 Tel
www.mousegate.com

ISBN: 978-1-59095-418-8
UPC: 6-43977-44181-2
Library of Congress Control Number:

Printed in the United States of America with simultaneous printings in Australia, Canada, and United Kingdom.

FIRST EDITION
1 2 3 4 5 6 7 8 9 10

To all the young readers out
there that still believe in magic.
Never give up on your dreams.

Award winning author Bob Doerr

grew up in a military family, graduated from the Air Force Academy, and had a career of his own in the Air Force. Bob specialized in criminal investigations and counterintelligence gaining significant insight to the worlds of crime, espionage, and terrorism. His work brought him into close coordination with the security agencies of many countries and filled his mind with the fascinating plots and characters found in his books today. His education credits include a Masters in International Relations from Creighton University. A full time author with thirteen published books, Bob was selected by the Military Writers Society of America as its Author of the Year for 2013. The Eric Hoffer Awards awarded No One Else to Kill its 2013 first runner up to the grand prize for commercial fiction. Two of his other books were finalists for the Eric Hoffer Award in earlier contests. Loose Ends Kill won the 2011 Silver medal for Fiction/mystery by the Military Writers Society of America. Another Colorado Kill received the same Silver medal in 2012 and the Silver medal for general fiction at the Branson Stars and Flags national book contest in 2012. In addition to Stranded in Space, Bob has written three prior novellas in the Enchanted Coin series: The Enchanted Coin, The Rescue of Vincent, and The Magic of Vex Bob lives in Garden Ridge, Texas, with Leigh, his wife of 46 years, and Cinco, their ornery cat.

Acknowledgement

I would like to thank all the young at heart who enjoy reading about magic and fantasy.

The Book

Stranded in Space: Book 4 in The Enchanted Coin Series is a 31,000 word fantasy adventure targeted at Middle Grade readers. Imagine being a fourteen year old again and finding a coin that seems to give off a light of its own. The coin has your name on it, claims to be magical, and instructs you to toss it into a fountain next to the Tree of Life. That's what happens in *Stranded in Space,* and what starts my protagonist off on a magical adventure that many young boys and girls would love to have.

This book is "G" rated.

Characters

Drake Thompson is a 14 year old boy, who finds an enchanted coin and is transported onto a damaged spaceship belonging to a race of people known as the Krozans.

Baya is a 14 year old girl from the planet Shantell who is also sent by a magical coin to the same spaceship at the same time as Drake. She looks like an Earth girl but her skin and hair are blue.

Zane is a Krozan teenager whom Drake and Baya have to bring out of hibernation to help them save the spaceship and the Krozan crew and passengers.

Introduction

Would you believe in the magic of a coin you discover that has your name inscribed on it? The coin claims to be magical and even has instructions for you to follow. Would you follow them? What if you did? Would you expect anything to happen? That's what happened to Drake Thompson. He found the coin and followed its instructions. What happened to him was totally unexpected and quite frightening. It led him to an adventure that many might think impossible to believe, but it did.

You be the judge.

Chapter 1

$\mathcal{D}$rake jumped back at the sight of the snake. "Fred! Get back here! He'll bite you," Drake said to his dog, a pudgy, brown and white bulldog that didn't seem to be the least afraid of the long, black snake that remained motionless on the ground.

"Is it alive?" Drake asked his dog.

Fred, of course, ignored the question. Drake gave another tug on the leash, and Fred returned to Drake's side.

"Let's see, Fred, no rattles so he's not a rattlesnake. He doesn't look like a copperhead because he's black, or a coral snake, either. I guess it could be a water moccasin, but we're a long way from any river or lake."

Remembering his phone, Drake took it out of his pocket and took a picture of the snake. As soon as the camera app in the phone clicked, the snake slithered off toward some bushes.

"Woof," Fred barked but didn't try to chase after him.

"Let him go."

"Woof," Fred barked again, but this time Drake realized his dog's attention had been drawn to a shiny gold coin on the ground that had been hidden underneath the snake.

"Awesome," Drake said and started to pick up the coin. He barely had it off the ground when he dropped it. "Wow! That felt funny." The coin had produced a tingling feeling in his fingers. Curiosity overcame caution, and Drake picked up the coin again. "Look how shiny it is."

Fred, however, had lost interest in the coin and started sniffing the ground along the trail where the snake had gone.

"Hey, Fred, this coin has my name on it," Drake said but stopped talking while he read the rest of the words on the coin. "What in the world?" He read the words on both sides of the coin again.

On one side of the coin, he could read the words "Magic Coin number 17 of 51." On the other side, the inscription said "Drake Thompson - throw this coin into the fountain by the Tree of Life."

Drake had turned fourteen the week before and believed that fourteen-year olds were old enough to know there was no such thing as magic, but this coin had something about it that made him wonder. The coin appeared to produce a light of its own, and he felt what he imagined to be a soft electric current buzzing from the coin into his hand. Additionally, even though he knew he had never seen the coin before, it did have his name on it, and he had a strong feeling it belonged to him.

"This is crazy, Fred," but his dog didn't have any interest in the coin.

He put the coin in his pocket and started walking home. He thought about the coin all the way home and wondered where he could find the Tee of Life. He didn't think of the snake again until he walked into his house.

"How was your walk?" his mother said from the living room couch where she sat working on a needlepoint project.

Rather than mention the coin, he immediately blurted out, "We saw a snake!"

"A snake, wow, what kind was it?"

"Here, I took a picture of it," Drake said and handed her his phone.

"Where?"

"Oh, yeah," he said and took the phone back to pull up the picture.

His mother studied the picture. "I think it's a hog nosed snake, but I'm not sure. Your dad will know. Let's show it to him when he gets home."

"Okay, but I think I'll try to find it on the internet."

Drake's father owned a pest control company and was an expert on all types of bugs and animals. He knew his dad would know about snakes, but Drake's desire to search for the snake on the internet hid the true target of his internet search, the Tree of Life. He didn't know why he didn't tell his mother about the coin. Maybe he would tell her later.

The internet listed so many sites that referred to a Tree of Life it left Drake confused. He didn't believe that the silly coin was magical, but it couldn't hurt to toss the coin into the fountain either. But, where was the fountain?

CHAPTER 2

*D*rake's father came home in a very happy mood. He stuck his head into Drake's room, "Hey, Drake, I have a surprise announcement to make at dinner tonight."

"What is it, Dad?"

"Nope, not until dinner, it's a surprise" he said with a big smile.

"Did mom tell you that Fred and I found saw a snake today?"

"No, what kind was it?"

"I'm not sure, but we took a picture of it?"

"We?"

Drake grinned. "Well, Fred was there, but I took the picture." He showed the photo of the snake to his dad.

"That's a hog nosed snake. It's one of the good ones, so I hope you didn't hurt it."

"Nope, we were too afraid at first to do anything, but I went through the steps you taught me. I figured it was one of the good ones, so Fred and I left it alone."

"Well, it's best to leave them all alone, son."

"I know."

"Listen, your mom said dinner will be ready in a few minutes, so wash up and come down. I think she's making spaghetti."

"I'll be down in a minute," Drake said. He loved his mother's spaghetti. What a great day, he thought. Seeing a snake, finding a strange coin, and now his mom was making spaghetti. He didn't think it could get much better.

He took the coin out of his pocket and looked at it again. It didn't seem quite as shiny as it was earlier, but he thought that might be because he was indoors and not out in the sun. The smell of baked garlic bread coming from the kitchen reminded him to wash his hands and head to dinner.

"Guess what," his father said once they were all eating.

"You've kept us in suspense long enough, honey. Please tell us," Drake's mother said.

"We're going to Disney World in Florida next week."

"What? How did that come about?" his mother asked.

"The business won it. I didn't even know we were one of the finalists. Our company gets so many of these flyers from the different suppliers we buy stuff from that I ignore most of them. I wouldn't have even looked at this one but Sibyl ran it in to show me."

"Does everyone get to go?" his mother asked.

"No, only one family of up to five family members, and if you remember, Sibyl and her family were just there a few months ago. Steve is single and has no interest. They both said we should go, and I've never been. Want to go Drake?"

"Sure, Dad, that sounds awesome," Drake said. He hadn't said anything when his father first made the announcement because he had remembered that during his internet search, one of the sites mentioned a Tree of Life being at Disney World. He wondered about this coincidence, and for the second time since he discovered the coin, he wondered if the coin could be magical. "What about school?" he asked.

"Thursday is a day off, so you would only miss one day," his father said.

"So that's why you were so interested in looking at the calendar when you got home," Drake's mother said.

His father grinned. Some spaghetti sauce dripped down his chin, and Drake's mother reached over and wiped it off with her napkin.

"We have six weeks to use the travel voucher, but this is the best time for me," he said.

"Sounds great," Drake said.

"Doesn't leave us much time to get organized," his mother said.

"Piece of cake," his dad said, meaning it would be easy.

"Piece of cake," Drake repeated.

His mother laughed at the two of them. "That's because I have to do most the work to get ready."

"We'll help," Drake said.

After they finished dinner, Drake raced back to his room and to his laptop. He found the website that talked about the Tree of Life at Disney World. This had to be the right one. It was too big of a coincidence not to be. He pulled the coin out of his pocket and studied it. Although, he couldn't be sure, the writing on the coin seemed like it had faded a little, and he decided the bright shine that the coin had when he discovered it had also faded more, too. He thought about writing the message from the coin on a piece of paper but then decided he could easily remember the instructions.

For the rest of the week, Drake wondered what, if anything would happen, once he tossed the coin into the fountain. Would he get three wishes like the story about the genie in the bottle? He doubted anything would happen, but he couldn't help but wonder.

He did not tell his parents about the coin. He didn't know why, but for some reason Drake kept the discovery of the coin to himself.

The night before the family's departure to Disney World, his mother came into his room. "I got a very nice call from Mr. Franks today."

"My teacher?"

"Yes. He said your science project on space travel was one of the best he has seen in years. Your paper about the difficulties of traveling long distances along with what you said about black holes, worm holes, dark matter, and other things I don't understand really impressed him."

"It wasn't anything much."

"He also liked the model spaceship you designed."

"Anyone who has seen Star Wars could do it," Drake said.

"Well maybe so, but he was impressed, and so are your father and I." She smiled again at him before saying goodnight.

He had worked hard on his science project, and Mr. Franks call to his mother pleased him. However, Drake hadn't known his project had impressed Mr. Franks a lot more than any other student's project had in many years. Despite Drake's statement that anyone could have done it, he knew that what had seemed simple and even fun for him to do was beyond the capabilities of many of the other students, and those who did have the brains to do a similar project didn't have the motivation to do so.

Drake had been an avid reader since he turned eight years old. He read everything he could find about space travel, fact or fiction. He had even gone to a space camp and thoroughly enjoyed it. Next to tossing the coin into the fountain, he had already decided that visiting Space Mountain was his second goal at Disney World.

CHAPTER 3

The plane ride to Orlando, Florida, seemed to go on forever, despite only lasting two hours. When the pilot finally announced the plane had started their final descent into Orlando's international airport, Drake almost cheered.

"Excited?" his dad asked.

"Yes, very much. I've never been here before and both Gary and Glen have."

"So you're the last of the fearsome threesome to visit Disney World."

"Yep, and I'm tired of hearing all their stories and not being able to have any of my own," Drake said and instantly thought of the coin. Wouldn't it be cool if something did happen when he tossed the coin into the fountain?

The area around the airport had scattered rain showers, and Drake watched out the window as the plane maneuvered around them before landing.

"That's rain, Drake, the dark stuff you see falling to the ground over there and over there. It looks different from up here because you can see it distinctly against the clear air around it."

"I knew that, Dad. I think it's cool. Maybe I'll be a pilot when I grow up, since I don't think we'll have spaceships by then."

"Yeah, you're only about a hundred years too early for that, but being a pilot is a good goal. You could join the air force and become a fighter jet pilot."

"That would be awesome," Drake said.

Drake's mother was busy with a crossword puzzle and didn't join in on the conversation. She did, however, occasionally look over and smile at Drake.

The landing made Drake a little more nervous than he thought it would, but once the airplane came to a stop at the gate, he was back in high spirits. He followed his parents off the plane and to the baggage department where the three started talking about all the things they wanted to do during their vacation.

"Grab it, son," his father said and pointed to one of their suitcases that went by while they were talking.

Drake reached for it but missed it and had to chase after it by going around a cluster of other passengers who stood next to them. He reached the suitcase before it travelled too far away and pulled it off the carousel. When he turned to go back to where his parents were, he bumped into a strange little man with big bushy black eyebrows and a thick, bushy black mustache. His eyes looked too big to be real, and they stared straight into Drake's eyes.

"Don't forget the coin," the strange man said, and repeated it. "Don't forget the coin." The man then spun on his heels and marched away.

Drake stared at the man, too startled to say anything. He hurried back to his parents. "Mom, Dad, did you see that strange man?"

"What man?" his mother asked.

Drake turned and started to point, but he couldn't see the man anymore.

"What about him?" his mother asked.

"Oh, nothing, he just looked really weird."

"Well, some people look different, Drake, but remember that doesn't make them any less of a person. Don't stare at them and don't pick on them for being different. That's being a bully."

"Oh, Mom, I know that. You've told me that a thousand times."

"Okay, this is the last one, let's go," his father said and picked up a green suitcase off the carousel.

The three left the airport and boarded the shuttle bus that took them to their hotel inside the Disney World resort. Once they unpacked, Drake's mother announced that she was starving and that they needed to eat lunch at the hotel before they went anywhere else. Drake didn't want to eat first but didn't complain. He knew once his mother made a decision, even his dad had a hard time changing her mind.

"Can we go to the Animal Kingdom first?" Drake asked as soon as they sat down at a table in the restaurant.

"Of course, anything in particular you want to see?" his mother asked.

"Everything!"

After lunch they went back to their room.

"Isn't it nice that this hotel is inside the Disney World Park? We can travel everywhere on their trains or buses," his mother said.

"But we aren't going to stay in the room right now, are we?" Drake asked.

"No, no, don't worry. Your father and I are just going to change, and then we'll go. You don't have to change," she said.

His parents disappeared into the bedroom of the hotel suite, and Drake sat down on the couch and pulled the coin out of his pocket. He studied the coin again. When the door to the bedroom opened, he looked up to see his parents come out of the room in matching shorts and tee shirts.

"Mom," Drake said. "Don't you think you're a little too old for that?"

His mom's shirt said Minnie and his father's had Mickey written across it. "Nope, and yours says Goofy."

"Oh, mom. Can I wear it tomorrow?" Drake asked.

"Okay. You'll really be impressed with the shirts we have for tomorrow. I make a perfect Snow White," she said.

"Embarrassing," Drake said. They all laughed and left the hotel.

An hour later, Drake and his parents were strolling around the Tree of Life discussing how large and amazing the tree was. While he walked, Drake searched for a fountain and had almost given up when he saw a small fountain that looked like it had been ignored by the maintenance crew for years.

"I'll be right back, Mom. I'm just going to walk over there for one minute."

"Okay, we'll be right here."

Drake walked over to the fountain and reached into his pocket. He felt the coin and pulled it out to look at it one more time before tossing it into the fountain. He wondered if he was just being silly, but he had come this far. He tossed the coin into the fountain and watched it tumble, almost in slow motion before it hit the water. When it struck the water, a bright light momentarily blinded him, and he took a step back, shutting his eyes.

CHAPTER 4

"What?" Drake said. He closed his eyes again and reopened them. He looked around confused and frightened. "Mom! Dad!" he shouted.

Everything had changed. He no longer saw crowds of people, the small fountain had disappeared, and he definitely was not in Disney World. In front of him, he saw thick vegetation unlike any he had ever seen before. The bushes had a mixture of blue, red, and orange leaves. The grey dirt he walked on didn't look natural. Heavy clouds drifted a few yards above his head blocking the clear sky that had been there moments before.

He started to panic, but then he remembered the coin, and the thought of it calmed him down.

"It can't be," he said to himself, but here he was. Something definitely had happened when the coin struck the water in the fountain.

Remembering he had his phone in his pocket, Drake took it out and saw that the screen was blank. He tried turning it on and off, but nothing happened. He put it back in his pocket.

"I must be in some strange country, maybe the rain forest in South America," he said out loud. He felt a drop of rain land on the top of his head. Looking up, he didn't see any more rain falling, but the clouds appeared dark and thick enough to produce a lot of rain. He hoped it wouldn't. Dressed in his blue jeans, white tennis shoes and a light green, collared tee shirt, he had not dressed to be out in the rain.

Drake looked around and tried to see something that might tell him to go in a certain direction, but he didn't see anything that indicated the presence of a village or even a single house nearby. He glanced back down at his feet and realized the grey dirt on which he stood was part of a trail that led through the bushes. He hadn't noticed it at first, because the plants had overgrown most of the trail.

He took a step then stopped, remembering his father once telling him that the best thing he could do if he ever got lost would be to stay put until someone found him. No, a thought came to him, he wasn't lost. The coin had sent him here.

"Is that possible?" he asked himself. It couldn't be, yet he knew that's exactly what happened.

He started walking down the trail. The bushes were so thick he had to move slowly and protect his face from a patch of thorny branches. After a few minutes, the bushes thinned out, and he could see clearly for about the length of a football field before more bushes closed in on the trail.

He continued walking and for the first time noticed what appeared to be a flock of birds flying above him. He didn't actually see the birds, but he heard what sounded like a flock of birds, and when he looked up he could see blurred images race by an inch or two inside the clouds.

"Hello! Anybody out there!' he shouted.

"Hello," a faint voice came from somewhere ahead.

Drake wondered if he what he heard was an echo of his own voice. It could have been, he thought, except what happened to the rest of what he said? Happy to hear someone else, Drake started running down the trail.

"Hello!" the voice sounded closer, but this time it came from his right.

Drake stopped and wondered if he should get off the trail. The trail had to lead somewhere, but if he left the trail and started wondering around in the jungle-like vegetation that surrounded him, he may never find his way back to the trail.

"I'm over here!" Drake called. "I found a trail."

"Me, too. Stay where you are, and I'll be there in a minute."

Relief flooded over Drake. He did not like being alone in this strange place.

"Okay, I'm in a clearing."

"I see you."

Drake turned his head a little and looked up the trail where it faded into the foliage. He saw her staring back at him. For a moment he didn't believe his eyes, and then he wondered if she might be experiencing the same surprise. The thought made him smile, and that, too, surprised him.

"I'm Drake," he said trying to break the ice. She might look different, but in a strange way, she might also be the prettiest girl he had ever seen.

"I'm Baya," she said, pronouncing it like Bay-ya. "Where are we?"

"You mean you don't know?" Drake asked thoroughly confused.

She took a couple of steps toward him. "Why do you look like that?"

"You mean the color of my skin?"

"Yes, it's different. I mean I've never seen a person like you."

"Well, not to be impolite, I've never seen someone with blue skin and blue hair before." A wild thought popped into Drake's mind. "Are you from Earth?"

"Where? No, I'm from Shantell."

"Shantell? Is that the name of the world where you're from?"

"Yes."

"How can this be? How did we get here?" Drake asked.

"Maybe we're both dreaming."

He hadn't thought of that. Could he be dreaming? "I don't think so. Look, I cut my finger back there." He held up his finger and showed her the small scratch.

"I don't think we're dreaming either. It must have been the coin," Baya said.

"The coin? Did you have one, too?" Drake asked.

"So, we both did. That proves it. But you couldn't have thrown yours into Lake Espeth."

"No, I've never heard of Lake Espeth. My coin told me to throw it into a fountain by the Tree of Life at Disney World."

"What is this Disney World, I thought you said your world was called Earth," Baya said. "Did you have to travel to a different world to use your coin?"

"No, it's just the name for a large amusement park. I never left Earth, except maybe now. Are we on your planet, Baya?"

"No, my world doesn't look anything like this. I don't know where we are, but we're not on my planet."

"I guess the important question is how do we get back to our homes? My mother and father will panic if I'm gone for long," Drake said.

"Mine will, too," Baya said, "but I think the more important question is why did our coins send us here?"

"I haven't thought about that. Do you think the coins sent us here for a specific reason? I guess that might be, but I can't imagine what we are supposed to do."

"I think we were sent here for a purpose, but I don't know what it could be either. Did your coin have your name on it?" Baya asked.

"Yes, did yours?"

"Yes, and it said it was enchanted."

"Mine said it was magical, but I guess that means the same thing," Drake said.

Suddenly the ground started shaking under their feet and a loud rumbling and cracking sound erupted around them. Baya fell to the ground, and Drake crouched down beside her.

CHAPTER 5

The shaking and the noise lasted only a few seconds. Large drops of rain fell around them for about ten seconds after the shaking stopped.

"Are you okay?" Drake asked. He reached over and offered Baya a hand.

"Yes," she said and grabbed Drake's hand to pull herself up. "I think we should find some shelter before the rain starts again."

"Which way?"

"Both of us arrived here next to this trail, and we both started walking in the same direction. I only came back when I heard you, so maybe we were supposed to continue in that direction."

"Sounds good to me," Drake said and the two began walking in the same direction they had been.

Baya took the lead and walked a few paces ahead of Drake. She kept a fast pace, and Drake might have complained back home, but he was too fascinated by her and their situation to say anything. Other than being completely blue, she looked human. The dark blue of her hair matched her fingernails, but contrasted with her lighter, sky blue skin. She wore a pair of beige slacks, a black short sleeve sweater, and sandals that were wrapped tight to her feet with small leather straps. She looked about his height, five foot seven, and like him, average weight for a person her size. She even spoke English.

"Hey, wait a second," he said.

She stopped and turned around.

"How do you know my language?"

"What? Oh, that's a good point, but you're speaking my language," Baya said, "I'm not speaking yours."

"How can that be? We're not even from the same planet."

"If the magic in those coins was strong enough to send us both here, I don't think it would take much more to allow us to speak to each other. Whether we are now speaking your language or mine, the fact is we understand each other, and I imagine we can thank the coins for that."

"It must be the coins," Drake said in agreement.

"I think the coins have done more than just let us talk to each other. I should have been terrified when I first found myself here, and while I did feel a little frightened, I never did feel that scared."

"I thought the same thing. The coin must have helped, but I think meeting you is what really calmed me down, Baya. I would really hate to find myself here alone."

"Well, since we're stuck together now and have nothing to do but to keep walking, tell me a little about yourself," Baya said.

"There's not too much to say. I'm fourteen, I live in Illinois with my parents, I guess I like school, and other than chores at home and playing with my friends, I don't do much else."

"Do you have any brothers or sisters?"

"No, but we do have a pet dog, named Fred," Drake said.

"Interesting," Baya said. "When you said pet dog, I understood the word pet but not the word dog. I had an idea, but I think I didn't understand it because we don't have dogs on my world."

"How about cats?"

"Nope," Baya said. "Do you have skots, bots, or nollots?"

Drake laughed. "No, they sound funny. Are they pets?"

"Yes," Baya started giggling.

"So, tell me about yourself."

"I have six sisters and brothers and live on a farm next to Lake Espeth. Like you, I am also fourteen years old. I like to climb and to run. Oh, I am also tall for my age." Baya said.

"Wow!" Drake said, not at Baya's remarks but at the view that suddenly appeared ahead of them.

"What a beautiful little lake," Baya said. "I like the red flowers floating there."

The thick vegetation they had been walking through ended, and for several hundred yards in front of them and to both their right and left, a lake with a sandy shoreline and beautiful blue water blocked their path. A large patch of what looked like red water lilies floated close to shore in front of them.

"The trail disappears in the sand," Drake said.

"I hope that doesn't mean we need to start swimming. I like to swim, but I can't swim all the way across the lake," Baya said.

"I don't think we need to. If we walk around the lake we should be able to find where the trail starts on the other side."

"Sounds like a plan. You know, something doesn't look right out there."

"What do you mean?" Drake asked.

"I'm not sure, but where the vegetation ends out there," Baya pointed to their right, "there's nothing and it's the same over there." This time she pointed to their left.

"Maybe it's just desert, and besides with these clouds so low, maybe they're blocking our view," Drake said.

Baya nodded, still staring at the horizon to their left, but didn't say anything.

"At least we can see trees on the other side," Drake said pointing in front of them.

"Which way around the lake?" Baya asked.

"Let's go that way," Drake said and pointed to their right.

They left what remained of the trail and started walking on the sand.

"Do all the people in your world look like you?"

"You mean my color?" Drake asked.

"Yes?" Bata said.

"No, the people in my world have different skin colors, but none are blue or have blue hair."

Baya grinned at him and placed her hand next to his, studying the difference. "Everyone on my planet is blue." When she pulled her hand away, she looked around. "How long do you think we'll be here?" she asked, changing the subject.

"I have no idea. I was wondering a little while ago how we're supposed to get back home. The magic in the coins sent us here, but we don't have our coins anymore." The thought of being stuck here on this strange planet sent a little shiver down Drake's back.

"I think the coins sent us here to do something, and once we've done it, the coins will take us back home."

"You must be right," Drake said, although he didn't feel very confident.

Suddenly, the lake made a gurgling sound and a large bubble of water swelled up in the middle of the vast lake. It collapsed sending a large wave out in all directions.

"Wow, look at that," Drake said.

"We'd better move away from the shoreline," Baya said as she started to jog away from the water.

Drake followed her, keeping an eye on the large wave racing toward them. It crashed against the shoreline just as they reached the edge of thick bushes and vines. The water turned from a deep blue to a light brown where it churned the sand. The forward motion of the wave slowed as the wave fought its way up the shore. By the time the water reached them, it could only wash up to the soles of their shoes before disappearing into the sand or returning to the lake.

"That was frightening," Baya said. "Our lakes don't do that."

"Neither do ours," Drake said as a thought came to his mind. A large water park, not far from his home, had a big swimming pool that could make its own waves, but this lake was a hundred times, no, maybe a thousand times larger than that pool.

"We would've gotten soaked if we stayed down by the shore," Baya said.

"The force of the wave would have knocked us down," Drake said. "It might have pulled us back into the lake."

"I wonder if there is anything dangerous in the water," Baya said.

"I don't want to find out," Drake said.

CHAPTER 6

"We've been walking for long time," Drake said. "We should see the trail again soon."

"So you haven't enjoyed talking to me," Baya joked.

"That's not what I meant. I've enjoyed talking to you. You're cooler than the girls back on earth." Drake's face reddened a bit when he said this.

Baya smiled. "I've enjoyed learning about you. We don't go to schools like yours, and we don't have winters like you described, but our world is not so different than yours. Maybe that's why the coins selected one person from both of our worlds to be here together."

"Do you think this has ever happened before? I mean like someone from our two planets being selected by the coins and sent somewhere together?"

"Not that I've heard of," Baya said. "But no one will believe me if after I return, I tell them what happened. I guess if it did happen before, and the person told people about it, nobody would have believed her either."

"Like the stories about UFO's," Drake said.

"Ha! We have those, too, but I've never heard about an enchanted coin."

"I imagine that right about now back on Earth, my parents are calling the police. They must be freaking out. I wish there was some way I could let them know I was safe," Drake said.

"Mine won't worry about me until tonight when I don't show up for dinner. Do you think we'll be sent home by then?"

"I hope so, but why are we here?" Drake asked. "I think we need to look for a sign or a clue that might help us figure out what's happening."

"Look at that!" Baya pointed out at the lake and grabbed Drake's arm.

A black tubular object broke the surface of the water just beyond the shoreline. Both of them jumped back, and the object disappeared under the water.

"It looked like the tentacle of a large octopus or maybe a huge snake" Drake said.

"I'm not sure what it was since we didn't see either end of it, but I hope it doesn't come ashore. Whatever it was, it's big. Can we run?"

"Sure," Drake said, and they started running. "Wait!" he shouted after a few seconds. "We just ran past the trail."

Baya stopped and seeing the trail hurried to it. "Let's get away from the water."

Drake followed her and the two walked several paces before Baya looked back at him. "Sorry, but that thing kind of freaked me out," she said.

"Me, too," Drake said. "This whole thing has me freaked out. Hopefully, we'll run into someone soon who can tell us where we are and why we're here."

They started walking again side by side as the trail widened. The thick bushes came to an end, and the terrain around them looked more like a forest, except the trees didn't look like trees on earth. The trunks had white bark that looked painted and artificial. The limbs of the tree all pointed upward and each tree seemed to have far fewer limbs than what Drake would have expected back on Earth.

"Do you have any special skills or powers?" Baya asked.

"No, I'm pretty ordinary. Why?"

"I was just wondering why the coins selected us. I don't have any special skills either. What if we aren't supposed to return to our worlds?"

"No offense, I like being with you, but I hope to go home soon," Drake said.

Baya grinned at him. "What if you get sent back to my world with me?"

"I'd rather go to your world with you than be left here alone. That's for sure. What is this?" Drake asked as they came to a clearing with what looked like dozens of large tables scattered about.

"Looks like big picnic tables," Baya said.

"But no chairs," Drake said.

"And no people, I wonder where everyone can be? Look over there," Baya said and pointed to their left. "It kind of looks like a playground."

"Maybe," Drake said, "but they must have tall children."

"Everything is bigger here than on my world, so maybe this is a planet where the people are all much taller than us."

"That makes sense. Let's hope they like strangers."

"I hadn't thought about that," Baya said. "By the way, isn't it getting darker?"

"Now that you mention it, I think so. With all these clouds, we can't see the sky, but it is definitely getting darker. I hope we find someone or someplace to stay before it gets too dark."

They continued down the trail that took them through the

middle of the large picnic area. A faint rumble of thunder echoed in the distance.

"That's all we need," Drake said, "being stuck out here in the middle of the night in a thunderstorm."

"This is crazy," Baya said and started giggling. "What else can go wrong today?"

Drake grinned and almost started laughing but stopped when a loud shriek came from somewhere high above them.

"What was that?" Baya asked, no longer giggling.

"It sounded sort of like a hawk, and a large one at that."

"Maybe we should run?" Baya said.

"I think so, too."

The two teenagers started running. They hadn't gone far when it became too dark to see the trail. At Drake's suggestion, they slowed down to a walk, so they wouldn't accidently get off the trail and get lost.

"I think I see a light ahead," Baya said.

Drake looked but didn't see anything. A light rain started to fall on them.

"It's faint," Baya said. "It's straight ahead, and I can't be sure because it's so dark, but the path might take us right to it."

"I see it now," Drake said after they got a little closer. "I hope it's attached to a McDonalds, I'm hungry."

"What's a McDonalds?"

"Oh yeah, where I come from they're restaurants. Actually, it doesn't have to be a McDonalds, as long as it's a place where we can get out of this rain and get something to eat."

"I'm not hungry, but I hope we'll meet someone there who can tell us where we are. Do you think they'll know why we are here?" Baya asked.

Drake instantly thought of the stories of Area 51 where the government supposedly kept outer space aliens that they captured. He had never believed the stories, but what if the people living here did something like that. Then he thought of the Men in Black movies. At least they treated space aliens better in that movie, and he and Baya would be considered space aliens to the people on this strange world.

"What if no one lives on this planet?" Drake said.

Baya didn't answer. The light flickered in front of them.

"Don't go out," Baya said, and started to run toward the light in spite of the darkness. Drake followed after her, and despite the periodic flicker the light remained on.

They stopped a few yards from the light.

"What do you think?" Baya asked.

"It looks like a fluorescent light that has had some type of plant grow all around and over it. I don't see any wiring or switch to turn it on or off. Of course, it's too high for us to reach anyway."

"It looks like a wall."

"A wall?" Drake said. "You're right. Thick bushes on either side that seem to go back a ways from us, but right here, we have a metal wall that runs up straight into these thick clouds and is about nine feet wide."

"Why the light, and why does this path lead right to it?" Baya asked. She walked closer to the wall and studied it. Drake came up next to her. After a moment, Baya reached out with her right hand and pushed against a small bump that Drake barely noticed.

Whoosh! A door in the wall slid open, and two teenagers jumped backwards. The open door exposed a well-lit hallway that led away from them for about thirty yards before it opened into what looked like a room or another hallway.

"I guess we're here," Drake said, his voice sounding a little higher than normal.

"Wherever here is," Baya said. "Let's go in."

Drake started to say that it might be better to wait a few minutes for someone to welcome them, but another hawk-like screech from somewhere close by changed his mind.

"Yes, let's do," he said and took a few steps inside.

Once they had both entered the hall, the door slid shut behind them with a heavy metallic clicking sound.

"This is definitely a hall and not a tunnel," Drake said.

Several feet above them, a series of lights kept the hall well lit. The walls and ceiling were composed of a shiny stainless steel-like material. A few black knobs fastened to metal rods protruded from high up on the wall to their right. The knobs had some symbols written on them in white, but Drake couldn't tell what they meant.

The surprises didn't stop there. When Baya and Drake reached the end of the hall they found themselves in another, wider hallway that ran both to their right and to their left for as far as they could see.

"This is strange," Baya said. "Why build a long hallway when we could have simply followed a trail outside."

"I don't know why, but we'll stay dry in here and away from any creatures. At least, I hope we do. Which way?"

"How about this way," Baya said, now facing left. "I think I see another intersection or a room down there."

"Okay, let's go," Drake said.

"How far do you think we've walked since we arrived?" Baya

asked a few minutes later.

"From when we met each other, a couple miles at least, but without a way to tell time, it could be longer." He looked behind them. "I can't even see the entrance to the hallway that we came out of. Who would build such a long hall? Maybe it's a passageway or a tunnel through a mountain."

"That makes sense," Baya said.

Just then the floor under them shuddered for a few seconds, and a loud metallic grinding sound echoed around them.

CHAPTER 7

"*I* hope that wasn't an earthquake," Drake said.

"Maybe we should hurry," Baya said and started to run. Drake hurried after her.

"Seems like all we've been doing since we've arrived is walk or run. How about we slow down and take a look in there," Drake said as they came to a short hall to their right that led into a room.

"Hello!" Baya shouted, but no one answered. "Let's go in."

Drake led them into the large room. "Wow, look at these. Think they're statues?" he asked."There must be fifteen or twenty of them."

Baya touched one of them. "They're carved out of stone. They seem to represent symbols of some kind, but I don't know what the symbols mean."

"Interesting, and there are similar paintings on the wall over there," Drake said. The paintings were not in frames but rather painted right on the wall.

"What's in there?" Drake said and started walking to an alcove. "Is this a window?" He reached up and touched what looked like a heavy curtain. As soon as he touched it, the curtain moved upward disappearing into a slot in the ceiling and exposing a large curved window. He looked out the window and said, "Baya, come here."

He was too surprised and fascinated by what he saw out the

window to notice her approach. She touched his arm.

"This can't be," she said. "It's impossible." Her grip on his arm tightened.

"We're on a giant spaceship," Drake said. Out the window he could clearly see thousands of stars in the distance and two nearby planets. One of the planets looked the size of a quarter and the second, farther away, looked smaller. For all he knew both planets could be larger than Earth, since he didn't know how far away they were.

"Look how big this ship is," he said. Drake could see portions of their ship behind them and in front of them. Stretching to put his head close to the window, he could also see what he thought was part of the ship several hundred yards below them.

"How could we have come in from outside and now find ourselves on a spaceship?" Baya asked. "Do you think we were inside the ship all the time?"

"I think we must have been. As big as this ship looks out this window, we could have been in a part of the ship used to grow food, create oxygen, and provide a place for the passengers to relax. I've read books about ships like this."

"But those books weren't true were they?" Baya asked.

"No, they were science fiction."

"Does your world have any large spaceships like this?"

"No," he said.

"Neither does mine," Baya said. "We travel to a couple nearby planets, but our ships only hold twenty to thirty people. We could fit our entire space fleet inside that space we were in when we thought we were outside."

"We haven't sent any people to the other planets in our solar system," Drake said, "and I don't think we even have a space fleet. Do you have any idea where we are?"

"If you mean do I recognize the planets, no. This could be anywhere in any galaxy, and we discover more galaxies every year."

"And every galaxy has millions of stars," Drake said. "We're definitely moving," he pointed out the window, "see, those planets are getting smaller."

"Why in the world would the coins send us to a spaceship? Can you pilot one of these or fix a broken engine?" Baya asked.

"No, of course not."

"Well, I can't either, and as big as this ship is, it could take us a year just to find our way around it."

"What are you two doing here?" a voice surprised them.

Baya and Drake grabbed at each other and both backed against the window. They looked around and, at first, didn't see anything. Then what Drake mistook for a metallic coffee table slid across the floor toward them.

"You two do not belong here. Who are you? Why did you come here? Why don't you speak the same language?" The table thing stopped about six feet in front of them. Drake noticed a small dome, the size of a cereal bowl and made out of light blue glass, situated on top of the table thing. The dome emitted a dull light, and the thing's voice seemed to come from it.

"We don't speak the same language?" Baya asked. "Why do you say that, and how do you understand us?"

That would not have been the first question Drake would have asked, but now that Baya had asked it, he did wonder why this table thing said it. Baya and he understood each other, and while a rare word she said he might not understand, overall he thought she spoke pretty good English.

"I'm programmed to understand all languages and dialects. In our universe, there are thirty-two different languages and forty seven dialects within those languages. Why without me and those like me, the Krozans would have extreme difficulty communicating. However, I have never heard your languages before."

"Then how did you understand us?" Baya asked.

"I'm not sure, but it must be in my programming," the table thing said.

"Or maybe it was the coins," Drake whispered to Baya. She nodded.

"What are you?" Baya asked.

"Me? Why I am a chittle. I help the Krozans communicate with each other on the ship and with other ships and worlds. I am also linked to all the ship's operations, not that that does any good right now. How may I address you?"

"I'm Drake, and this is Baya."

"Why are you here?" the chittle asked.

"We thought you might be able to tell us that," Drake said.

"Me? I don't know why you were sent here, unless you came here to help us," the chittle said.

"Why do you need help?" Baya asked.

"Oh, things are bad, things are bad." Immediately after saying this, the chittle moved to the nearest wall, stood up on two legs and pressed itself against the wall. All four legs, which were each about two feet long, somehow retracted into the table top.

"Were we just talking to a table?" Drake asked.

"Yes," Baya said and walked closer to the chittle. "I can't see anything on it. It's just hanging there."

"I'm starting to think this is all a crazy dream."

Baya smiled. "Dreaming about me, that's flattering."

Drake grinned. "How did it move?"

"Maybe little wheels on its legs. I think it's some form of a robot. Unless you have a better idea, I suggest we wait here for a while and see if it will talk to us some more."

Drake looked around. "Sounds like a plan. When it talks, it sort of sounds like my grandfather. What is this?" He walked over to a corner of the room. "It looks like a pile of blankets." He felt it. "Soft. If we're going to wait, we might as well do so in comfort. I think we need to rest a little anyway. You can have a couple of these."

Baya came close to him. "I am tired. It must be night time back home." She looked around the room. "Do you think it's safe?"

"I think so. That table, or chittle, has been the only thing that's communicated with us so far. I think we should stay here for a while." He picked up more of the blanket and tried to pull it apart. "This appears to be one very large blanket. I guess we could share, if you don't mind, or I could go over there." He pointed to the far corner of the room.

"I don't mind, plus we need to talk some more," Baya said. "What do you think he meant when he said that things are bad here?"

"It could mean anything. Here, take this end of the blanket."

"It is soft," she said as she stretched out part of the blanket. She sat on it and pulled a portion of it over her legs. "Where are these Krozans the chittle mentioned? I got the impression they are the people that operate the ship, so why haven't we seen any?"

"I'm sure we'll meet them soon. Have you done any space travel?" Drake asked.

"No, but I may go to college on Stane, that's the planet next to ours. The government operates a shuttle for students to get back and forth. Space travel is expensive, and my parents can't afford it. Most of the people who travel in space belong to the science council or are the crews of the large commercial ships that take raw materials back and forth. Not many people can afford their own ships or pay for seats on one of the transport vessels."

"Wow, that's still awesome. We don't have anything like that. Only a few people from my world have ever been in space, and we haven't had anyone travel to Mars, our neighboring planet."

Baya said, "We've been travelling to our neighboring worlds for a long time, but we haven't travelled outside our solar system. Of course we've sent out unmanned ships for science purposes, but it takes a lifetime to reach the nearest neighboring solar system, and the few unmanned ships the space agency sent out have failed."

Baya fascinated Drake. He even liked listening to her talk, and he had never been one to care what girls said back home. He felt comfortable with her, like he had known her for a long time. How strange, he thought. He closed his eyes not intending to sleep, but within a minute he was sleeping.

Baya looked over at Drake and noticed he had fallen asleep. Unlike Drake's lack of interest in girls, she had been interested in boys for a few years. Baya even knew one boy, Zell, whom her parents teased her about, calling him her boyfriend. She thought Drake would be handsome with blue skin and blue hair, but she had already become use to his light brown skin and curly brown hair. No one where she came from had naturally curly hair.

She wondered why she wasn't more afraid, or why she wasn't thinking about her parents or Zell. Her parents had to be worried about her, but for some reason Baya felt everything would be alright. The magic from the coins must have helped her from becoming too frightened, but she also thought Drake's presence helped a lot.

Baya looked over at the chittle and saw that it hadn't moved. She thought she would stay awake for a while in case something happened, but like Drake, she soon fell asleep. Neither of them saw the chittle slide off the wall and approach them.

CHAPTER 8

"*H*ello! Hello! Hello!"

Drake and Baya opened their eyes and sat up.

"Recharging time is over. Spending too much time recharging is inefficient. Rule 74, rule 74."

"Wait a second, Mr. Chittle, let us wake up," Drake said.

Baya stretched. "You've named him. I like it. Mr. Chittle, is that what you were doing on the wall, recharging?"

"Of course. I am allotted five hours each cycle to recharge, not that it matters now, not that it matters."

"You said that before," Baya said. "Why doesn't it matter now?"

"The Krozans stopped functioning, and now the systems are all shutting down."

"What do you mean the Krozans have stopped functioning? Are they dead?" Drake asked.

"Not yet but soon."

"What happened?"

"Something happened, yes, something happened," Mr. Chittle said.

"But what?" Baya asked.

"I'm not sure. I can communicate, but I have limited memory. The explanation was too large for my memory."

"Like a computer, is that what you are Mr. Chittle?" Baya asked.

"Oh, I am much more than a computer."

"Of course you are," Drake said realizing that Mr. Chittle had emotions. "We are new here and don't understand everything. "Can you tell us what you do know about what happened to cause the Krozans to stop functioning?"

"Of course I can."

Drake grinned thinking of the number of times his mom corrected him by saying: can I or will I. "I mean please tell us what you can about what happened."

"Our ship collided with a very powerful stream of radioactive particles, a gamma ray burst. We had only a few seconds to react before the collision, not enough time to prevent serious damage to the ship. Fires started, and toxic gases spread throughout the ship. The captain confined all nonessential passengers and crew to quarters. It became worse, and everyone had to wear safety suits. Most of the fires were put out, but the damage to the ship damaged the air filtration system and the toxic gases continue to spread. Finally, all but a handful of the crew had to seek shelter in their hibernation suits."

"Is that where they are now?" Baya asked.

"Yes."

"You said all but a handful of the crew. Do you know where they are?" Drake asked.

"No. All contact ended."

"When?"

"Two years ago."

"Two years ago," Baya repeated. "How could that be? Shouldn't you have arrived at your destination by now? Has no one tried to rescue you?"

"We dropped out of hyper speed when the collision occurred.

We drifted off course, and all ships communications stopped."

"How far were you from your destination?" Drake asked.

"Not far, maybe a month at hyper speed. At our current speed, one hundred and twelve years," Mr. Chittle said. "Of course, that would first require a direction change."

"That's a big difference," Drake said.

"I do not know if a ship has been sent out to find us," Mr. Chittle said. "Navigation from one solar system to another is not hard, but within the empty space between the two solar systems it is very hard to find anything."

"Why is this ship traveling from one solar system to another?" Baya asked.

"The Krozans are establishing a colony on Pylex Prime. It is the only planet that we have found that has the right environment for the Krozans. This ship took the original colonists there. A second ship has also transported colonists to Pylex Prime."

"We saw two planets out the window before we fell asleep. Are you sure we couldn't be there already," Baya asked.

"The ship had to pass close by two other stars with their own planets on its journey. I suppose the planets you saw were in one of those solar systems."

"That's amazing that the Krozans can travel between stars. Have they ever been to Earth?" Drake said.

"I do not know where this Earth is. There are millions of stars in our galaxy and millions of other galaxies. I do not think the Krozans have charted any other planet besides Pylex Prime that can host life, but they have only charted eighteen solar systems," Mr. Chittle said."I need to take you to the command center, but I'm not sure how we can get there."

"What is the command center?" Baya asked.

"It's where the pilot flies the ship. You might also call it the ship's bridge."

Drake stretched his arms, "Why don't you know where it is?"

"I know where it is, but we have to go through the damaged areas to get there, and I don't believe we can go around two of those areas."

"Still, I think we should try," Baya said, and looking at Drake added, "I think we were sent here to help. We have to try."

Drake nodded.

"The command center computer agrees with you," Mr. Chittle said.

"What? You can communicate with the command center? It would be good if we could talk directly to it," Baya said.

"You will be able to talk to it if we get to the command center. It can speak like me."

"Can you lead us there?" Drake asked.

"Yes, like I said, there would be no problems if we hadn't had the accident." Mr. Chittle started sliding across the floor and out the door. Drake and Baya followed it.

"I must caution you about the command center computer," Mr. Chittle said. "It's a bit obnoxious. It thinks it's superior to the rest of us just because it has a bigger memory. We don't think it's any better than us, and neither do the laydrops"

"What are laydrops?" Baya asked.

"Have you not met a laydrop yet? Come to think about it, I haven't seen one in what, let me think. Oh yes, oh yes, I haven't seen one since the accident."

"Are they okay?" Baya asked.

"Yes, we still communicate, but they went to try to extinguish the fires. The laydrops are designed to handle maintenance and repairs."

"What are the chittles designed to do?" Drake asked.

"We are specialists in administration. Would you like to see some of my skills?"

"Of course, Mr. Chittle," Baya said.

The chittle stopped, and the entire table top lit up like a computer screen. It flashed a series of charts and diagrams.

"Impressive," Baya said.

"I can also be taller," the legs suddenly extended to a point where that table top was six feet tall. "Or, I can become a wall desk." It slid over to a nearby wall. Once one edge of the table top touched the wall, the two table legs nearest the wall shortened and folded up under the table. The edge of the table touching the wall slid upwards a foot.

"What a nice desk you make," Baya said.

Drake smiled and wondered why Baya was giving the chittle so many compliments. He considered the possibility that Baya saw Mr. Chittle as a living creature rather than a strange looking robot.

"Thank you," the chittle said and started leading them down the long hallway again.

They passed several connecting hallways and dozens of rooms containing a variety of strange furniture.

"What are these rooms, Mr. Chittle?" Drake asked.

"Most of them are classrooms and meeting rooms. This is a long voyage and the students must continue their studies. This entire section of the ship was abandoned after the accident. Oh, I do miss the little ones," Mr. Chittle said.

"The first section of the ship we visited was a large area that looked like we were outside of the surface of a planet. We saw trees, plants, and a large lake," Drake said.

"That is one of the two relaxation parks on the ship. That one is a favorite of the younger Krozans. I have never seen it, but the children like to tell me about it."

"Mr. Chittle, why haven't we seen any other chittles yet?" Drake asked.

"Most of the chittles have been turned off to conserve their battery and memory life. We were not designed to operate continuously. The Krozans will be impressed with how long those of us who were left on have lasted."

"But don't you recharge each time you need to?" Drake said.

"Yes, but we always have a complete diagnostic and reboot every three months. I have no record of any chittle going beyond that three-month schedule. The Krozans are very serious about their schedules."

"How many chittles did they leave operating like you?" Drake asked.

"I don't know. We are all connected, so I know other chittles are still operational, but I can't tell how many. I know one is waiting for you above us."

"Above us?" Baya asked.

"Yes, the elevators are not running and the ramp near here is damaged, so I won't be able to go up with you. But you must, if you are to reach the command center."

Mr. Chittle stopped next to an opening in the wall to their left that disclosed a steep, circular ramp.

"The ramp doesn't look damaged," Baya said, walking over to the ramp. "Oh, now I see. How are we supposed to get up there?"

Drake joined her and looked upward. "That looks like it goes on forever."

"You do not have to climb to the top, only five levels. A chittle will meet you there. He says the railing is not far from the deck on that level and even a baby Krozan could make the jump."

"The jump? I don't know, Baya. Can you climb up that railing?" Drake asked.

"I'm a good climber. This shouldn't be hard, and if it's the only way to get where we need to go, let's do it." Without saying another word, she walked up the ramp as far as she could and climbed onto the dangling steel hand rail where the ramp ended.

Drake followed, thinking that he would never try this if he were alone. The steel railing seemed secure, but the lengthy space between the individual rails forced Drake to stand on one rail and stretch to reach the next. He had to let go of the handrail that now went straight up before reaching up and grabbing the next cross rail above him. He then had to pull himself up with his arms while wrapping his legs around the hand rail to support his climb.

Drake repeated this process several times before he heard a loud rumble and the railing began to shudder and sway. He tightened his grip and looked up. Baya hung from a cross rail and appeared to be swinging back and forth. Drake thought she must be trying to get her legs back around the handrail, but suddenly she appeared to lose her grip and slipped off the railing.

"Baya!" he shouted.

CHAPTER 9

"I'm okay," Baya said. "Hurry up! I don't like that sound."

She made it, Drake thought. She climbed a lot faster than he could, but the fact that she was safe and had reached the correct floor encouraged him to keep climbing.

In less than a minute, he climbed the rest of the way to her, but an empty space five feet long still separated him from Baya and the safety of having a solid floor under his feet.

"You'll have to swing back and forth until you can let go and fly to the deck like I did. I don't think the railing is stable enough to let you stand and get a good jump off it," Baya said.

Drake had already realized the same thing. Normally a five-foot jump would be easy for him, but the railing swayed just enough to make it impossible to push off of it and jump. He didn't like the idea of swinging by his arms and then letting go, but he also knew he didn't have much of a choice. The rumbling started again and the railing shuddered.

"Hurry," Baya said.

"Yes, you must hurry," the chittle next to her said. This one looked exactly like the chittle they had left below.

The vibration in the railing worsened. Drake grasped the cross rail above his head and started swinging back and forth. As he did, the shaking in the rail made it difficult to maintain his grip. He looked down and saw the end of the railing break loose. Dust and other debris fell through the air around him. He kicked his feet out trying to get as much momentum as he could. His feet swung away from Baya and had started in their arc toward her when he heard a loud crack.

"Now!" Baya yelled.

His feet swung toward her, and in the fraction of a second before he intended to let go and let his momentum carry him to the safety of the solid deck, something gave above him and the railing started to collapse. Drake let go, but because the steel rail he held on to had already started to fall, he wasn't able to use his shoulders and arms to control his flight through the air. The top half of his body fell backwards even as his legs moved through the air toward safety. Just as his feet struck the floor, he felt a hand grab his and pull him to safety.

"Are you okay?" Baya asked. She sat next to him where she had fallen while pulling him toward her. She still held on to his hand.

Drake sat up and realized both of them were only inches from where the floor ended. He looked over the edge and saw the pile of railing five levels below them. "Thanks," he said to Baya and gave her hand a gentle squeeze. "I'm okay."

"We must go," the chittle said. "Time is running out."

"What do you mean?" Drake asked.

"Power to the Krozan life support systems has stopped. The backup system will not last long," the chittle said.

"Does that mean we will lose the air we breathe, Mr. Chittle?" Baya asked.

"No, the power that maintains the hibernation pods has been cut, not the power to the ship's life support systems," Mr. Chittle said. "We must hurry."

"Then I guess we should go," Drake said, standing up. He let go of Baya's hand and was surprised at his desire to hold it again once they started walking. Instead, he said, "So, this one is also Mr. Chittle. What will do if we see two of them together?"

"If we do, you'll have to give them first names," she said and grinned.

"You're teeth are white," Drake said.

"What? You just noticed?"

"No, I must have noticed, but, oh, I don't know," Drake said. "I guess it's just another thing we have in common."

"Blue teeth would look weird," she said, and they both laughed.

"This hallway looks like the one we were on below," Drake said. "Do all hallways look alike, Mr. Chittle?"

"They are supposed to look alike, but many are damaged now and look different."

"How can you tell what floor, I mean which deck you are on?" Drake asked.

"Each deck is marked."

Drake looked at Baya and then back at the walls. "I don't see anything."

"I don't either," Baya said.

"There along the floor." Mr. Chittle said.

They looked where the floor and side walls met and saw a series of symbols.

"Can you read that?" Drake asked.

"No," Baya said.

"I guess it doesn't matter as long as we have a guide," Drake said. "Mr. Chittle, how far do we have to go to get to the command center?"

"The distance is not great, but the challenges are many and

dangerous."

"Dangerous," Baya said.

"Yes there are fires up ahead," the chittle said.

"If the fires started long ago when the ship collided with the radiation, why haven't they burned themselves out by now?" Baya asked.

"The fires are fed by a series of fuel leaks, and we will never run out of fuel as the ship constantly regenerates new fuel," the chittle said.

"So, are the fires getting worse?" Drake asked.

"The laydrops are putting the fires out almost as fast as the new ones are starting. The number of fires is not much higher than it was a year ago, but each time a new fire erupts more of the ship is damaged. The laydrops are losing power and many have been destroyed. They cannot spend any more time repairing the ship, because they have to fight the fires."

"How much of the ship has been damaged?" Drake asked.

"Eleven percent."

"That doesn't sound too bad," Baya said.

"The center of the ship is where the Krozans live. It is the most shielded part of the ship. The water, food, and fuel regeneration systems are also there. The collision caused minor damage in that large part of the ship and no fires. The outer layers of the ship suffered significant damage."

"Mr. Chittle, can you display a current picture of the ship on your screen?" Drake asked.

"Of course I can. I have the capability to display any part of the ship. What would you like to see?"

"Show us what the ship might look like from outside the ship?" Drake said.

A large-scale picture of the outside of the ship appeared on the table top.

"Wow! That's an odd-looking ship," Drake said. "It looks like a fat octopus with short tentacles. Except, the ship's tentacles come out from all over the main body of the ship."

"I've never seen anything like this either," Baya said.

"This is what I believe the ship looks like now," Mr. Chittle said.

The picture changed to display sections of the ship that had been damaged or destroyed. Drake thought the ship now had a two or three missing tentacles and had a number of cracks along the ship's hull. The picture slowly rotated giving Drake and Baya a complete picture of the ship.

"Where are we?" Baya asked.

A red dot lit up the screen. "We are here and we need to go there," Mr. Chittle said. A yellow dot appeared.

"Doesn't look too far away," Baya said. "Is it on this level?"

"No it's seven levels above us."

"I hope we don't have to climb any more railings," Drake said.

The chittle didn't answer him but started moving again.

"I'm getting hungry," Drake said as they followed their guide.

"Me, too," Baya said. "I wonder what type of food they have here."

"Mr. Chittle, is there any food on this ship that we can eat?" Drake asked.

"Of course, the Krozans have many fine delicacies. We are not far from a place to eat. It is on our way."

"Think we'll like it?" Baya whispered to Drake. She scrunched her nose and made Drake smile.

"I hope so. Say, Mr. Chittle can you show us a picture of a Krozan?"

"Of course, male or female, old or young?"

"A young adult," Baya said.

A picture showed up on the table top screen that made both Drake and Baya take a step backwards.

"This is Pootoe. He is considered a handsome male. Would you like to see a female, or someone less handsome?"

"No thanks," Baya said. She looked at Drake and whispered, "Not very attractive."

"Looks like a fish that has evolved over the centuries to have arms and legs. No neck and even a fish like tail that must drag on the ground behind him," Drake said.

"And a grayish white skin that looks bumpy. I'm glad the coin sent you here rather than someone like that," Baya said.

"I guess we're being a little harsh. He could be very pleasant," Drake said.

"I know, and we've been taught that it's not how one looks but rather their behavior that matters. But still, seeing him was a bit of a shock."

"It was, and I'm happy the coin sent you. Other than our different colors, I think we are alike."

"I don't know about that. Are boys and girls bodies alike on Earth?" Baya teased.

"No, of course not, but you know what I mean," Drake said looking away.

"I'm not sure I do," Baya said as she walked a little faster getting a few feet ahead of Drake, so he couldn't see the grin on her face.

CHAPTER 10

"The eating room is right here," Mr. Chittle said and turned into an open room to their right. It stopped in the middle of the room.

The room looked similar to the one where they first met the other chittle. Statues and pictures on the wall decorated the room. Drake looked around for a window but didn't see one in this room. "How do we get any food?" he asked.

"You can instruct the automated nutrition and drink system to provide you what you want, but since you are not familiar with the ship, I can do it for you. What would you like to eat?"

"Do you have a menu?" Baya asked.

"No, everyone knows what's available," the chittle said.

"Please order whatever is the favorite meal of the Krozans?" Drake said.

"I guess for me, too," Baya said.

"I have done so. Your food will be here shortly." Without further comment, the chittle slid over to the nearest wall and pressed its table top against the wall, folding its legs up against the bottom of the table top.

"I guess it's recharging. Who would design a robot that looks like a table? It's kind of lame," Drake said.

"Our robots are designed to look like us," Baya said.

"That at least makes sense."

"I guess it's efficient though. You need tables and desks, and you need computers and robots, so I why not combine them all into one?"

"Good point," Drake said. "How do you think our food will show up?"

"Guess we'll have to wait and find out," Baya said. "I'm more concerned how it will taste than how it arrives."

They heard a grinding sound and a large section of a nearby wall slid upward and revealed a counter. On the counter sat two large bowls. They walked to the counter and standing on their tip toes, looked into the bowls.

"Uh oh," Baya said.

"Maybe it won't be too bad. It looks sort of like a bowl of dirty water with a partially stirred up raw egg floating around in it. I think it's cold, too." He picked up the bowl and smelled the contents. "I can't smell anything."

"You go first."

"Okay," Drake replied and seeing that they had no spoon, took a sip. "It doesn't have any taste. If I hadn't seen it, I would think I was drinking room temperature water. In fact, I wish I hadn't seen it."

Baya tasted the liquid then took a bigger sip. "Not bad, not good, but not bad."

Both drank a little more of their soup-like meal. Neither drank the entire contents. Suddenly, Drake burped. "Oh my gosh, that burned." His stomach cramped for a second, and he thought he might get sick, but another loud burp erupted from his stomach, and just as suddenly, he felt better. He stood still for a second not willing to move.

Next to him, Baya tensed and covered her mouth with her hand. "Ugh, I've been poisoned," she said. She bent over and remained motionless for about four seconds before standing upright. "Next time, let's order something different."

"Are you okay?" Drake asked.

"I am now, how about you?"

"I'm fine. How long do you think Mr. Chittle will be?"

"I don't know," she said and sat down on a long flat cushion that lined an adjacent wall. "Drake, these Krozans are obviously more advanced than either of our worlds. They are larger and most likely stronger. I can't imagine how we can be of any help to them."

"Maybe they only need us to pull a switch or a lever. The chittles can't grip anything. Maybe none of the robots have the ability to grab a knob or a handle and move it," Drake said.

"But they seem so automated. Why would they need levers that would need to be moved by hand?" Baya asked.

"Maybe as an extra layer of backup in case everything else fails," Drake said.

"Could be," Baya said. "Couldn't the magic coin just fix it and not bother us?"

"Then you wouldn't have met me?" Drake said and smiled.

"And I wouldn't have had the experience of eating some of the Krozans' favorite food," Baya said.

"Oh, man, you're not comparing me with that poison, are you?"

Baya grinned.

"I don't think we'll ever really understand how and why the magic in the coins did what they did. I mean, if they needed someone to come here and fix a problem, why not send one person right to where the problem is and guide that person to the solution? I mean we just appeared here with no clue and no warning," Drake said.

"Maybe magic isn't supposed to be logical. You know, we're doing a lot of walking, and I have a feeling our trip is going to get a lot more dangerous soon. Drake, do you think the coins will keep us safe. I mean, I know we don't have them with us, but I believe their magic is with us, otherwise how could we understand each other or the chittles?"

"I think the magic is still with us, and I think it will get us back home safely," Drake said, but he had his own doubts and worries.

"Drake, why do you think they picked a boy and a girl? Why not two boys or two girls?"

He started to say he didn't know, but then the word chemistry came to mind. "Maybe the coins simply picked two people and it ended up one of each, or maybe the coins thought a boy and a girl might get along better than two boys."

"Or two girls," Baya said. She grinned and Drake was about to ask her what she was thinking, when the room shuttered and they heard an explosion in the distance followed by a loud cracking sound as a nearby wall cracked open. Dust flew around and everything went dark for a second before the lights came back on.

"What was that?" Baya asked.

"Not good, not good," Mr. Chittle said, arriving next to them from his position on the wall.

"A fire!" Drake exclaimed and pointed to the new opening in the wall. A flickering light could be seen in the distance.

"The fire is spreading again. Not good, not good," Mr. Chittle said.

"Do we need to go?" Drake asked.

"Yes, we must. I know where," Mr. Chittle said and slid out

the room into the hall. The two teenagers followed it. "This way, I must take you to the laydrops."

"How far away are they?" Drake asked.

"Not far, not far," the chittle replied.

After walking for fifteen minutes, Baya said, "I think his definition of not far is different from mine."

Drake nodded. "I agree. I like to play sports, but if we keep walking too long, I'm going to be worn out. You must play sports too, Baya, you don't seem to be getting tired at all."

"I like to run and climb. We have a small mountain near my home that my friends and I are always racing to the top."

"Wow, up a mountain, that's impressive. That's why you are in such good shape," Drake said.

"You like my shape?" Baya asked.

"No, I mean you don't tire out," Drake answered embarrassed.

"So, you don't like my shape?"

"No, I didn't say that either." He stopped talking when he saw her smile and realized she was teasing him. "Girls," he said and shook his head.

"I wonder why we haven't seen or smelled smoke," Baya said.

"That's a good question. Mr. Chittle, why don't the fires on the ship produce smoke?" Drake asked.

"They do, but the ventilation system cleanses the air. This ship's system is very modern and most efficient." Mr. Chittle said.

"It sure is," Drake said.

"Still it took over a year to get the air back to normal. All five of the power stations that run the ventilation system survived the collision with the gamma ray burst. Most of the food and water processing were unaffected, too. However, as the fires spread these systems are now being damaged, too," the chittle said.

"Too bad the ship didn't have better firefighting capabilities," Baya said.

"The laydrops are extremely efficient, but the initial damage was near catastrophic. Our engineers and scientists were surprised that we survived the initial impact. None of our smaller ships would have. The odds of any ship being struck by a random gamma ray burst are less than a million to one."

"That is bad luck," Drake said.

"Uh oh," Baya said as they rounded a bend in the hallway.

Ahead of them, the walls and ceiling had collapsed into one jumbled mess, preventing them from walking any further.

"What are we supposed to do now?" Drake asked.

"This must have been caused by the last explosion. We must continue," Mr. Chittle said.

"Do you have robots that can come clear the hall?" Baya asked.

"No."

Drake walked up to the pile and started pulling pieces of twisted metal off and away from the pile. "I think we can clear this. The metal is surprisingly light."

Baya came up next to him and grabbed a piece of metal. "I know the coins sent us here for some reason, but if I could snap my fingers and go home right now, I would."

"And leave me alone?"

"Of course not, I'm assuming we could both go back to our worlds."

"Good," Drake said.

It took a half hour of pulling and lifting, but finally the two teenagers cleared a path wide enough for the three to continue on. However, upon inspection of the far side of the debris pile, they realized that the hallway floor had fallen into to a large pile of debris two decks below them. The walls and ceiling had collapsed with it, leaving only a few metal beams that connected this end of the existing hall with the far end where the floor, the walls, and the ceiling appeared to be intact once again.

"I think we can get across on this beam," Baya said and grasped the beam next to them.

"Think it's strong enough?" Drake asked. "The beam is only three to four inches wide."

"I think so," Baya said. "Mr. Chittle can you make it across on the beam?"

"No, it would be impossible, but another chittle is coming to the other side right now to help you the rest of the way. You must hurry. The command center has told me that there is not much time left before the backup power to the life support pods quits."

"I'll go first," Baya said. Before Drake could even comment, Baya jumped on the beam and scooted across to the other side while sitting on the beam with her legs straddling it.

Drake climbed on the beam and crossed it in the same manner as Baya. When he reached the far end, he discovered getting off the beam and onto the floor was harder than it looked. The beam reached the edge of the undamaged hall, but where the beam went into solid wall, he had nothing but emptiness below his feet. In fact, he had to scoot back several inches to give himself enough space to climb off the beam. He reached out with his left foot and touched solid floor, but that left the rest of his body leaning on the beam and staring down into nothing but air for about thirty feet to where a pile of debris had settled. How did Baya get off so easily?

"Here, grab my hand and push off the beam with your other hand," Baya said.

Drake looked down and fought off the panic that tried to get him to stay on the beam. Grasping the beam with his right hand and keeping his extended left foot on the floor, Drake took Baya's outstretched hand in his left hand. He pushed himself up a few inches with his right hand and swung his right leg over the beam. For a second it seemed that his weight would cause him to crash back onto the beam, but he pushed himself toward the solid floor.

After a second, he felt his center of gravity shift onto his left foot, and with Baya's help he found himself standing on firm flooring.

"That was the hard way," Baya said.

Drake felt a little embarrassed and started to reply when Baya continued talking.

"You must be very strong to push yourself off the beam with one hand and then to continue to push yourself. I could never have done that."

Drake's embarrassment vanished. "You helped. Thanks. How do you make everything look so easy?"

"I've been climbing for my whole life. We all climb. It comes naturally to us. We develop a feel for how to move about from branch to branch or ledge to ledge. It's second nature to me."

He had an image of the family of squirrels that lived in the trees by his house jumping from branch to branch. He smiled and decided to keep the image to himself. After all, Baya certainly didn't look like any squirrel he had ever seen.

The two looked back across the gap at Mr. Chittle.

"Should we keep going or wait here?" Drake said.

"Keep going. You must hurry," the chittle replied.

CHAPTER 11

They hadn't gone far when they saw a familiar object approaching them from the other direction.

"Mr. Chittle, we are sure glad you're here. We need help getting to wherever it is on this ship we are supposed to go," Drake said.

"Yes, yes, I will lead you," the chittle said.

"You think it's possible that there is only one chittle?" Baya whispered.

"You mean that each of the chittles we've seen could be the same one?" Drake said.

"No, I assure you that there are three hundred and eighty-seven of us still functioning aboard the ship," Mr. Chittle said.

Baya raised her eyebrows and smiled at Drake. "You have good ears, Mr. Chittle."

"I do not have ears, but we are designed to hear all sounds at all frequencies."

"How many chittles were functioning on board before the collision with the gamma ray burst?" Drake asked.

"One thousand and three. The initial collision destroyed over half of the chittles and a fourth of the laydrops."

"That's a lot," Baya said. "Why were more chittles affected than laydrops?"

"The laydrops have extensive shielding. Only those directly hit by the gamma ray burst were damaged or destroyed," Mr.

Chittle said.

"When will we see the laydrops?" Baya asked.

"Soon," the chittle said.

Drake looked at Baya and then at the chittle. "Does that mean we're nearing the part of the ship that is still burning?"

"Yes, it is near. You will have to go with the laydrops when we reach that part of the ship. They know the command center needs your help, so they will keep you safe."

Baya said, "I hope so."

"How do you know how many chittles are still operating when the last chittle we were with didn't?" Drake asked.

"After you asked the question, we did an inventory," the chittle answered.

Suddenly everything went dark. Baya grabbed Drake's hand.

"Oh my," the chittle said.

The lights came back on.

"That is not good. The backup power units have gone offline, and the ship is now on battery backup power."

"How long will they last?" Drake asked.

"We do not know," the chittle replied. "It has never happened before."

"Then let's hurry up and go," Drake said.

The three started moving a little faster down the long hallway. In another ten minutes they reached the end of the hallway.

"Oh no," Drake said.

Baya didn't say anything but stared at the sight in front of her.

They both stared into a huge section of the ship that had been destroyed by what must have been a massive explosion. Mangled strips of metal hung from the walls above and around them, but most of what they saw was a vast emptiness. Small fires could be seen several levels above them and one could be seen far below. They saw strings of black smoke that appeared to be attached to spots on the walls above and below them.

"This is the only spot on this side of the damaged area where you can travel all the way to the other side," Mr. Chittle said.

"How is that possible," Drake asked.

"I believe it means on this," Baya said and pointed at a fairly large metal beam about eight feet away that bent upward and disappeared about thirty yards from them into a spot where a number of twisted metal beams appeared to have been tangled together by the explosion. While a few smaller beams and cables ran from the cluster back toward them, one metal beam shot out from the cluster and continued on to another cluster of tangled beams in the distance. From there it was impossible to see where it led.

"Where are the laydrops?" Drake asked.

"This one will go with you," Mr. Chittle said.

Drake looked up and was surprised to see what looked to him like a flying ball. At first, he thought the laydrop was floating in the air, but then he realized it had wings that fluttered so fast they were almost impossible to see. Bigger than a basketball, the laydrop appeared to be made out of a grey metal and had two slits in the metal that ran around it body like rings.

"Fascinating," Baya said as she also studied the laydrop.

"Can they speak like you?" Drake asked.

"No, but you just have to follow it," the chittle said.

"Can they hear us?" Baya asked.

"Yes. They have excellent hearing. The laydrops fix and repair things. They communicate with the command center if they need anything. Otherwise there is no need for them to talk to anyone.

We, on the other hand, advise and educate the Krozans and must be able to talk to them."

"Do you communicate with the laydrops?" Baya asked.

"Yes, we communicate with each other through the command center. We are on the same network," Mr. Chittle answered.

"Did the laydrops select this way for us to reach the command center, and if they did, why? It seems to be quite dangerous," Baya asked.

"The laydrops did recommend this route, but the central computer made the final decision. Usually, the command center computer only makes recommendations to the ship's captain or to other members of the senior staff, but since they are not available, the command center computer has taken charge, as it is designed to do in emergencies."

"Do you have many emergencies like this?" Drake asked.

"This is the first in our history. I'm sure the Krozans will study how well it performed once we are rescued," the chittle answered.

"I'm sure they will," Drake said.

"Is there any chance that there will be more explosions in this section of the ship while we are trying to cross to the other side," Baya asked.

"Yes, but this way was chosen because the odds of getting through are a lot higher than any of the other routes. The laydrops will keep you safe," the chittle said.

"Not very comforting," Drake said and wondered again why he wasn't more afraid than he was. Before he could spend much time considering this, Baya leaped across the open space to the beam and landed on it on her feet without any difficulty.

"It's stable and wide enough to walk on. From here, I can see that it would have been easier to reach the beam by using the ledge and the piece of the railing that hangs off that edge," Baya said and pointed to a section of the damaged ship next to Drake.

Drake leaned out and looked to his right. Along the damaged side he saw several places where he could place his feet and simply walk to the beam. The ragged side also had several spots where he could grip something to help maintain his balance until he reached the beam.

"Hurry now," Mr. Chittle said. "Once across, another chittle will take you the rest of the way."

Drake nodded and, hugging the damaged edge of the ship, stepped away from the solid flooring onto a ragged and broken ledge. Keeping a tight grip on various pieces of damaged metal, Drake walked slowly to the beam. He stepped on it and turning to faced Baya who watched him.

"I think we can walk on this," she said looking down at the beam.

Drake looked down. Big mistake, he thought, and he quickly looked back at Baya. Below the beam he saw nothing but dozens of mangled metal strips sticking out from the side of the damaged ship. If he fell off the beam, he would either collide with one of the metal strips or continue falling as far as he could see.

"Drake, we better go," Baya said and looked into his eyes.

"I'll be fine," Drake said. "The beam is about eighteen inches wide. I'll keep my eyes focused on you and the beam. I won't look down again."

They started walking out on the beam away from the undamaged part of the ship. They hadn't gone far before the beam bent upward toward the first mangled cluster of metal strips and beams. Drake found walking up the incline slower but easier than walking on the flat part. He didn't know why, but thought it was because he had to lean forward a little to keep his balance, bringing the beam closer to his face.

"We'll have to squeeze through and step over a lot of these other pieces of metal," Baya said, "but at least there are a lot of things to hold onto while we do."

Drake caught up with Baya as she squeezed through the first tight cluster of bent metal. She moved with the agility of gymnast, while he worked up a sweat reaching the far side of the cluster.

"It's a long way to the next cluster. Do you think we should we rest for a minute or start now?" Baya asked.

Drake saw the laydrop waiting for them about twenty feet away. "I think we better keep moving."

Baya led on and within seconds the two found themselves out in the middle of an open expanse. Drake tried to keep his eyes focused on Baya and the beam between them. A couple of times he caught himself stepping too close to one edge of the beam or the other and quickly moved back to the center.

"Stay straight," he said to himself.

"What?" Baya said without looking back.

"Just talking to myself. You would think it would be easy to walk in the middle of this beam, but I catch myself drifting off to one edge or the other."

"That's normal," Baya said, "the key is to get back to the middle without panicking. Staying calm is most important."

"This is easier than walking across the log above Richard's Creek back home," Drake said. "Except this is a lot longer and a lot higher and, of course, in the middle of a space ship."

"We have a long log that crosses above a creek back home,

too. That log wobbles when you walk on it, making it very hard to keep your balance. At least this beam is very stable," Baya said.

In the distance, he saw flames shoot out from what looked like a small fire. The fire instantly doubled in size. Watching the fire, he felt himself drift away from the center of beam. He looked back down and saw his right foot step on the very edge of the beam. He stopped and once again forced away the panic that wanted to overpower him. When he resumed walking, he hoped he could keep his focus on staying in the middle of the beam. Falling would mean certain death.

CHAPTER 12

Although it seemed like hours to Drake, they reached the second cluster of tangled metal only fifteen minutes after leaving the prior one. A long thick cable hung from a section of the ship way above them and appeared to support this cluster of metal pipes, beams, railing, and smaller cables.

Baya ducked under a thick metal bar and found a spot to sit inside the cluster. Drake squeezed in and sat next to her.

"Even though they don't talk, it's a comfort to have it out there," Baya said, looking at the laydrop that hovered a few yards away.

"The chittle said they repair things and put out fires," Drake said. "How do they do anything? Can you actually see their wings? I just see a blur."

"I can't see their wings either, but I guess the fluttering blur we see must be their wings."

"Like a bumblebee," Drake said.

"Like a what?"

"It's a bee that we have on Earth that has a big body and small wings. People think bumblebees shouldn't be able to fly because of their small wings, but somehow they do," Drake said.

"Like the laydrops," Baya said. "We'll have to wait to see them in action to find out how they can fix anything."

"I wish they could deliver a pizza," Drake said. "I'm hungry again."

"Me, too."

"We have a choice of two beams leading away from this cluster. It's a good thing we have a guide," Drake said, pointing at the one on their left.

"I think it wants us to go on that one. Should we go?" Baya asked.

"I guess so. We're supposed to be hurrying."

The two teenagers resumed their walk across the open expanse. Drake thought they had reached the middle because when he paused to look around, the damaged but solid walls of the ship in front of him and behind him seemed equally far. This time he didn't lose his balance when he looked around. In fact, he had become quite calm despite the situation he was in.

"Think we should walk a little faster?" Drake asked. "Our laydrop appears to be getting farther ahead of us."

They started walking faster, and Drake looked off to his right and saw that the beam that they didn't take ended in mid air. If they had selected that beam, about now they would be turning around and retracing their steps back to the cluster.

"Another cluster of mangled metal ahead, and then it looks like we'll be close to the other side. I'll be happy to get off this beam," Baya said.

"I can't wait," Drake said. "Although, I feel like I have gotten used to it. I was all stiff and nervous walking on the beam to that first cluster back there, but after that it's not been bad."

"Look over there," Baya said and pointed ahead and to their left. "See the laydrops?"

"Yes. It looks like they're fighting that small fire, but I can't see how they are doing it. When we get closer, maybe we can."

"That fire is far enough away that it shouldn't bother us,"

Baya said. They could see the yellow flames against the grey background of the ship and a stream of smoke that seemed to be attached to the side of the ship.

"You can see where the ships ventilation system is sucking in the smoke," Drake said.

"I'm amazed that the ship held together with such a large section of it destroyed. This whole empty space we've been walking through used to be part of the ship. On my planet we could fit an entire space ship inside here," Baya said.

"We could fit every space ship we have on Earth in here," Drake said. "When we get to the other side, we'll have to ask a chittle to display this damaged section within a picture of the entire ship so we can see how much of the ship it covers."

"Good idea. We may have to climb through and over this cluster to get to the other side," Baya said as they approached this final tangled web of metal. She did not hesitate and began climbing over the pieces of metal.

Drake followed her, thinking it wasn't much different than climbing across some of the playground "monkey bars" he used to play on when he was younger. They moved quickly, but this cluster was a large one. Drake saw two large cables that supported the cluster along with the beam on which they had been walking. The cables ran diagonally upward to the interior section of the ship where the damage from the explosion stopped.

He also saw a large beam stick up out of the cluster they were on. The beam shot straight up about fifteen feet before the broken jagged end of it curled like a candy cane back towards them.

Baya passed near this beam when a loud explosion rocked the entire ship. Drake watched as a piece of the ship the size of his house back on Earth blasted out into the open space a hundred yards away, break into several smaller pieces and fall toward a giant pile of debris several hundred yards below them.

In a second, fire shot out of the opening left behind by the explosion. Small flashes of what looked like lightning also streaked out of the opening. One such streak of electricity raced across the damaged wall of the ship in front of them. This streak disappeared and a large cracking sound followed it. Drake saw a dark line caused by the electricity extend from where the explosion occurred to a point next to where one of the large supporting cables connected to the wall. Before the danger could register in Drake's mind, disaster struck.

It happened fast, but to Drake it seemed like it was all slow motion. The end of cable broke away from the ship, and the cluster he was on collapsed inward about a foot before tilting to the right. Several pieces of metal fell out of the cluster, causing the cluster to again collapse a few inches. A piece of metal Drake was holding onto started to slide away, and he had to quickly grab a different piece. Smoke filled the air around him, and he coughed and closed his eyes.

"Baya! Are you okay?" he shouted. She didn't answer him. He opened his eyes and saw that the smoke was already being drawn away from them. He also saw seven or eight laydrops darting in and out around the area of the explosion. Two laydrops hovered in the air near him.

Drake looked for Baya and at first couldn't see her. He started moving to where he had last seen her. The pieces of metal he crawled over shifted positions and even slid away from him when he put his weight on them.

He saw movement close to him in the cluster and heard her. "Help! Drake!"

Moving closer, the realization of what happened scared him. The large beam had collapsed and looked like it had crushed her and the cluster of metal poles, rails, siding, cables and whatever else had been around her. A definite crease about a foot deep and the length of the beam ran across the cluster. The beam settled in and likely caused that crease. It looked like it had fallen right on Baya.

Drake crawled in close to Baya. Her eyes were open, but when she spoke, Drake could tell she was having trouble breathing.

"I can't move," Baya said.

Drake immediately began to pull the smaller pieces off her. As he did, he realized that the large beam had settled a couple inches above her chest. That was fortunate, but the beam had trapped a number of smaller strips of metal and pipes that now pressed on her.

The ship shuddered for a full two seconds, and pieces of metal in the cluster again shifted. Fortunately, the large beam didn't move any closer to Baya.

"I can't move. You need to leave me. I think this whole thing is going to fall. Please save yourself," Baya said in a gasping voice.

"I'm not leaving you," Drake said and continued to pull pieces of metal off her.

"You must. You can't move that beam."

Ignoring her, Drake cleared everything but three items off her. The beam appeared to rest on these three items. Two of the items reminded Drake of flag poles. They extended across Baya and continued into the cluster. The third item looked like a section of wall or flooring that had been ripped away during an explosion. About an inch thick and a foot wide, it also extended off to Baya's right side into the cluster. The other end of this piece of metal bent down and pressed in against the middle of Baya's stomach.

"I may not have to move the beam," Drake said to her after studying the situation. "The large beam is being supported by a bunch of different stuff. If I can move these three just a little I may be able to pull you out." Baya didn't respond, and when he looked her he saw that her eyes were shut. He grabbed her hand and was relieved when he felt her squeeze his hand.

He tried to lift one of the poles, grabbing it at a spot near Baya, but he couldn't budge it. He looked at the pole and how it extended past them and had an idea. In school earlier in the year, he had learned about the early tools used by humans. One of the tools discussed was the fulcrum. If he could find another pole he might be able to build a fulcrum.

Finding one was easy. The cluster contained hundreds of individual pieces of metal of all shapes and design. To finish building his fulcrum, Drake had to find a solid piece of metal on which he could rest the pole. Next, he found a spot on the cluster where he would place his fulcrum. He picked this particular spot because he saw that if he could lift the pole that pressed against Baya's legs just an inch, a large chunk of metal that had already slid next to the pole should slip underneath it. When he let the pole back down, the chunk of metal should be strong enough to keep the pole nearly an inch higher than it was.

The rod Drake selected for the fulcrum measured about eight feet long and nearly two inches thick. Strong enough for sure, he thought, but it was heavy. Drake placed the block of metal that he would use for the fulcrum's base on a solid slab of metal near the pole that he needed to raise off Baya. He lifted one end of the rod for the fulcrum and awkwardly placed the other end of it on the block of metal that now functioned as the fulcrum's base. He slid the fulcrum's rod forward a foot until it was solidly under the pole he needed to lift. The end of the rod he gripped angled upward. Holding tight to the very end of this rod, he lifted his feet and hung from it. Even though this put all his weight on it, nothing happened.

Determined not to give up, Drake braced both of his feet under a slab of metal to give him some leverage. He then pulled down on the pole with his arms using his weight and all the strength he could muster. He strained so hard a growling sound escaped from deep down in his chest. He heard a "thud," and somewhat to his surprise, he saw that his plan had succeeded. While he didn't see it happen, he had lifted the pole just enough that the chunk of metal slid underneath the pole.

He looked at Baya to see if the pole was still pressing against her. He couldn't see any difference from before, but believing the he had lifted the pole a little, he hurried next to her and tried to move her leg.

"Great! It worked," he said out loud. He could slide her leg back and forth a little. He tried her other leg and it slid even easier than the first. "Baya, we're going to get you out of here." She didn't say anything, and her eyes remained closed.

Drake grabbed the two pieces to his fulcrum and began studying the other long metal pole that ran across her lower chest. He couldn't find a spot like he had on the last one where a piece of metal leaned against the pole ready to slip under it. In fact, he couldn't even find a spot near Baya where he could rest the base of the fulcrum. Studying the situation, a possibility came to mind.

Rather than use the base he had used earlier, Drake saw a spot about two feet away from Baya where he could rest one end of the rod to his fulcrum and the slide it forward under the metal pole that pressed against Baya. If he could lift the pole an inch or two off Baya, he could then slide the rod forward about six inches and rest it on a wad of twisted metal. That twisted metal might be strong enough to hold the pole up enough to let Baya slide out from under it. He would lose the use of the rod he was using with his fulcrum, but he was sure he could find another.

He rested the end of the rod on the narrow strip of solid metal that would now serve as the base for his fulcrum. As planned, he slid the end of the rod under the pole that pressed against Baya's chest, and gripping the other end once again, he put all his weight on the end of the rod. This time he felt the pole lift a little, but, as he was hanging on the rod, he couldn't slide it forward. He gently let everything return to its original position.

Like before, Drake had to hook his right foot under some metal screening while he planted his left foot squarely on top of another piece of sheet metal. This time he hung from the end of the rod and pulled down with his arms. The rod lifted the pole. While still maintaining the downward pressure on his end of the rod, he slid the rod forward until it was in place. When he let go, the rod to the fulcrum did not move.

Scrambling back to Baya, he saw that there was now a good inch between her and this second pole. The large beam still rested on the two rods, but as it had been raised slightly along the two poles, it no longer touched the slab of broken flooring that rested on Baya's belly. Drake tried to lift the piece of flooring and discovered that he could, but with the beam still resting just above it, he realized he had to slide the flooring off her.

Gripping it under the curved end, Drake pulled it towards

him. The piece of flooring didn't slide easily, and as it did the metal pieces that sat on or rested against the flooring would shift at the far end. Something suddenly shifted and a small section of the cluster collapsed within itself. The overall cluster didn't move, but it frightened Drake. He decided he had pulled the slab enough. The curved end was no longer pressing on Baya.

He let the slab of flooring down and saw that it remained in contact with Baya. Lifting the end of the slab and holding it in place with one hand, Drake grabbed a nearby piece of thick metal cable and placed it under the curved edge of the flooring. When he lowered the curved edge, the one-inch thick cable was compressed about a half inch where the edge of the flooring sat on it, but it held.

"Baya," Drake said and gently shook her shoulder. "Baya, wake up."

Baya's eyes fluttered and then stayed open. "Why are you still here?"

"I think I can pull you out now, but I need you to help. You may need to move around a little if parts of you get stuck."

"Parts of me?" Baya asked.

"I'm mostly worried about your feet," Drake said.

Baya moved her legs and for the first time she realized that the metal rods no longer had her pinned. She squirmed and tried to wiggle herself free but didn't get very far.

"Hold on," Drake said. "Let me pull you out."

The task wasn't easy since they weren't on a firm surface like a floor. This part of the cluster, like the rest, consisted of twisted metal sheets, poles, cables, and the like. Most of Baya's body rested on what looked like part of a metal cage, and in some spots nothing supported her at all. Drake had to find a good spot to brace his feet each time he tugged on Baya. Finally, she slid free of everything.

Baya sat up and looked at herself. "I'm surprised I'm not cut up more than I am." She had a few tears in her pants and the lower part of her black sweater had a rip where the metal had pressed in on her. She started to stand but quickly sat back down.

"Are you okay?" Drake asked.

"Yes, just a little dizzy. We need to move on. I feel like this whole thing is going to collapse," Baya said.

Drake remembered she had said that before and wondered if she had some sixth sense. Either way, he was ready to get off the cluster, too. She started crawling across the top of the cluster before he could ask her if she needed help.

He followed her and they reached the large beam that continued on away from the cluster to the safety of the ship. Baya stood up on the edge of the beam, but collapsed back into a sitting position. For a second, Drake thought she might fall off the cluster and grabbed her as she sat down.

"I'm still a little dizzy," Baya said.

"Oh, I see why," Drake said. "You have nasty little swollen spot on the back of your head. Something must have hit it."

Baya reached up and rubbed the back of her head. "Ouch, that is tender. You go first, and I'll crawl after you. I'll be fine, and that way I won't hold you up."

"It'll take you forever to get across if you crawl. Let's wait here a few minutes and see if you begin to feel better," Drake said.

"Okay, but only for a minute."

He reached over and gave her hand a squeeze and she smiled back at him.

"How did you lift that beam off me? It must have weighed a

ton," she asked.

"I didn't have to lift the beam, just the two poles that it rested on. It wasn't easy, but I'm happy you're free. I would never have left you back there."

The ship shuddered again and debris started falling off the cluster. Drake heard what he thought was metal making a groaning sound ahead of them.

"We better go," Drake said, but when he looked at Baya her eyes were closed. Had she fallen asleep? He shook her gently and her eyes opened.

"I'm tired," she said. She didn't sound like she was worried about anything, and that frightened Drake.

"Come on, I'll carry you across," Drake said. With just enough help from her, he managed to get her on his back. He stood up on the beam and with Baya now on his back, he started across, carrying Baya "piggy-back" style. He moved slower than he could without her, but he kept a steady pace. She didn't seem heavy at first, but over time she seemed to get heavier and heavier.

The distance to the safety of the ship shrank, and for Drake it became a battle between reaching the safety at the end of the beam or having to stop and somehow take a rest with Baya still on his back.

"Baya, Baya, can you hear me," Drake asked, hoping she might be awake, but he received no answer.

Suddenly disaster struck.

CHAPTER 13

A small explosion erupted near where the last one had. The explosion barely caused the beam Drake stood on to shudder, but a second after the explosion Drake heard the loud sound of metal cracking. The crack that ran along the damaged inside surface of the ship from the spot of the explosion to the beam widened. The change in size of the crack seemed to only be an inch or two, but the damage was done. With a loud groan, the beam on which Drake stood started to pull away from the wall.

The movement of the beam was slight, but Drake definitely felt it. He also saw a small crack in the metal beam appear and stretch across it. He saw other cracks developing further ahead of him on the beam.

Two things happened immediately. First, Drake forgot his fatigue and started running with Baya still on his back. Second, six laydrops raced to positions next to the beam and started repairing the cracks. Each laydrop sprayed a stream at the cracks. The thin stream looked like a clear liquid as it left the laydrop, but by the time it reached the metal beam, it looked like a stream of molten metal. Their accuracy amazed Drake.

He could see steam rising from the beam as he approached. He tried to avoid stepping on the cracks, thinking that his shoes might get stuck if the sealant was some type of powerful glue. It also looked very hot.

Drake reached the safety of the hallway but didn't stop

running until he was a good ten steps inside and away from the beam. Breathing hard, he went down on one knee and let Baya roll off his back. He sat next to her, leaning back against the solid, intact wall and closed his eyes. A few seconds later, he heard a loud cracking sound and looking out into the large expanse from which he had just come, he watched as the beam broke apart near the closest cluster. The cluster seemed to sag in slow motion and then picked up speed as it plummeted down and away from him. The beam twisted to its right and tilted slightly downward but remained fixed to the ship as it extended out about seventy-five yards before coming to a jagged end.

"How did we get here?" Baya asked. She sat up next to him and rubbed her eyes and then her forehead.

"We're safe now," Drake said.

"Did you carry me?"

"Yes, I told you that I wasn't going to leave you," Drake said.

She looked back out to where the cluster used to be. "You saved my life." Drake didn't say anything, and Baya wrapped both her arms around Drake's right arm and leaned her head on his right shoulder. "Do you think we'll ever get to go home?"

"Yes, I do," Drake said and hoped he sounded more confident than he felt. "Here comes our guide." He watched as a chittle raced towards them.

"We must hurry," the chittle said. "Not far to go now."

"Can you walk?" Drake asked Baya.

"I think so," she said and with a little help from Drake, she stood up. She kept a hand on his shoulder, and he wrapped his arm behind her back and supported her as they started to walk behind the chittle.

Walking helped Baya get her second wind and clear her mind.

After a few minutes she let go of Drake and started walking on her own.

"Mr. Chittle, I hope we don't have to go through another damaged section of the ship," Drake said. "We almost died in that last one."

"Going through saved a lot of time. We are near the command center now," the chittle said.

"Good," Baya said. "Do you have any idea yet what we are supposed to do when we get there?"

"You will find out when we get there," the chittle replied.

"Why do I feel like we are going to visit the Wizard of Oz?" Drake asked.

"What?" Baya asked.

"Just a movie I saw. Doesn't mean anything," he said.

"It must have meant something," Baya said.

"It's a movie where this girl is trying to get to see the Wizard of Oz, so he can send her back home. She was sent to a strange world sort of like us. When she finally meets the wizard and despite what everyone has told her, she finds out he really doesn't have any magical ability to send her home."

"So how does she get home?" Baya asked.

"She had been wearing magical shoes all along. The shoes sent her back home. I guess that's not unlike our coins, except we don't have the coins with us anymore," Drake said.

"I'd like to be wearing magical shoes right now," Baya said.

"Me, too," Drake said, and they grinned at each other. Drake looked at his white tennis shoes and saw that the side of his left shoe had something gooey on it, and the shoe appeared to be burned along the edge of the goo.

They hadn't walked far when they entered a section of

hallway where the lights were out. The chittle's table top screen turned on and produced enough light so the two teens could follow him. They could also see the floor and walls near them.

"Why are the lights out here?" Drake asked.

"I don't know, but the power lines must have been cut. The damage to the power lines is what caused most of the ships problems and most of the cut power lines are right here in the area we have entered," the chittle said.

After walking for a few minutes in the dark, they entered a portion of the hallway where the lights worked again.

"This is better," Baya said.

"Yes it is," Drake said. "Mr. Chittle, can you display a picture of the ship and include where we are now and where we have to go?"

"Of course," it said, and the screen instantly displayed a section of the ship that had two red dots near the center.

"Do these red dots reflect the two of us?" Drake asked.

"No they reflect where we are and where we are going," the chittle said.

"Can you do a close up?" Drake asked.

The picture changed and the dots were now at the two ends of the screen. Drake could clearly see hallways running in various directions. They appeared to be in a hallway that led straight to the other red dot.

"It doesn't look like we're far from the command center or central doemmand or whatever it's called," Baya said.

"Not long now," the chittle said.

They started walking again, and after another fifteen minutes they came to a spot where a metal ladder attached to the wall on their left led up through a small opening to the deck above them.

"You must go up this ladder and another chittle will take you the rest of the way. Not long now," the chittle said.

"You've been saying that for a while now," Drake said.

"Yes, yes," the chittle said.

Without a second thought, Baya quickly climbed up the ladder. Drake followed her and found himself in a large room not unlike the few rooms they had been in before with weird looking statues and walls with a variety of paintings painted directly on them. What he didn't see was a chittle waiting for them.

He was about to shout down to the other chittle when Baya tapped him on the arm and pointed at the wall behind them. There fastened to it was a chittle apparently recharging.

"I guess we get a chance to rest for a while, too. I've lost track of how long we've been here, and I'm hungry again," Drake said. "Actually, I think I'm more thirsty than hungry."

"Me, too," Baya said. "When our chittle is finished recharging and wakes up, we'll ask it to fix us some food, and we need to be sure it's something different than what we had last time."

"Yes," Drake said and nodded in agreement.

"There's another pile of blankets over there," Baya said, pointing to a corner of the room. "I suggest we try to rest."

"Good idea," Drake said. "Although I can't wait to do whatever it is we are supposed to do to will help save this ship. I mean, that has to be why we were brought here."

"We agree on that, but, like I said before, I can't help but wonder what we can do. Maybe this central computer will tell us." Baya picked up a corner of one of the large blankets and wrapped it around her as she sat down.

Drake sat down next to her. She reached over and took his hand in hers.

"You are the bravest person I've ever known," she said. "I still can't believe you saved me. You could've died." She leaned back against the wall and closed her eyes.

Drake was glad she did because he didn't want her to see him blushing. He didn't think he was all that brave. How could he live with himself if he ran off and left her? No, he thought, if faced with the situation again, he would do the same thing. He would save Baya or die trying.

He wondered what his parents were doing. They would be frantic by now and would have gone to the police. When he returned to Earth, how would he ever explain what had happened to him? Nobody would believe him. Without meaning to, he fell asleep.

CHAPTER 14

"Drake, wake up," Baya said and gently shook him.

Drake opened his eyes and blinked a few times. Rubbing his eyes, he forced himself awake. "Oh, I was really asleep."

"Your food is ready," he heard the chittle say.

"Mr. Chittle woke me up a minute ago, so I ordered us some food and something to drink. We're trying something new." Baya walked over and took the tray off the shelf and brought it back to Drake. She sat down next to him.

"It looks like bread and what's this?" he pointed to a lump of what looked like pudding.

"Pudding," she said, and he grinned.

Baya used what looked to Drake like a spoon without a handle to scoop up some pudding and took a taste. "Not very good, but as hungry as I am, I'll eat some."

Drake tore off a piece of bread and put it in his mouth. "This almost has no taste at all, so I guess that's good."

Baya ate some bread and nodded at Drake. He used the second spoon and ate some pudding. He made a face and Baya laughed.

"This tastes like my dad's sardines. I didn't expect that." He had eaten sardines with his father for as long as he could remember. He had never really enjoyed the sardines, but he did like the fact that his father always invited him to share the sardines with him. He ate some more pudding and bread while thinking of his parents.

"Where is this command center?" Drake asked the chittle.

"Next door, but we are too late," the chittle said.

"What do you mean too late?" Drake asked.

"The command center computer is no longer working. All remaining power has been diverted back to the life support systems in this part of the ship," the chittle said.

"This part of the ship?" Baya asked.

"Yes, the part of the ship where the Krozans live," the chittle said.

"Mr. Chittle, how long will you be able to communicate with us?" Baya asked.

"Not long, and most of the chittles have already been turned off. The laydrops are still functioning."

"Can we enter the command center?" Drake asked.

"Of course," the chittle said and a door close to them opened.

The three entered the large room. Drake was amazed how similar the command center was to the ones in all the science fiction movies and television shows he had seen. He thought in the movies they referred to it as the "bridge". The first thing he saw, and what drew his attention was a large window through which he could see the front of the ship and out into space. The size of the ship once again amazed him.

"Beautiful, isn't it," Baya said, standing next to him. "I still can't get over how large this ship is."

Something to Drake's left caught his attention. "Oh my," he said softly. He walked over to two figures slumped over. The two figures still sat in tall chairs, but the upper half of their bodies rested against instrument panels directly in front of them.

"Are they Krozans?" Baya asked.

"Yes. The two are no longer functioning. They were the last

of the emergency crew. Poisonous gases seeped into their air supply," the chittle said.

"Did everyone's air supply go bad?" Baya asked.

"No, those in hibernation tubes have a separate system. They are still fine," the chittle said.

Drake barely heard the conversation as he was studying the two Krozans. They appeared to be about eight feet tall, but he couldn't be sure since both of them wore spacesuits that were made out of something that looked like aluminum foil, though he guessed that the suits were a lot stronger than aluminum foil. He looked closely at the face of one of the Krozans and stepped back.

He could only see part of the face since the suit covered most of it. A transparent, glasslike material about eight inches long and two inches high stretched across the Krozan's eyes allowing Drake to look in.

Baya brushed by him and peered in. "I find it interesting that you, I, and the Krozans are so similar."

"Similar?" Drake said.

"Yes, we all have two eyes, two arms, two legs, walk upright and live in large civilizations. We all seem to be intelligent, and we all have a desire to travel in space."

Drake understood what she meant. He hadn't thought about it, but what she said was correct. "I guess the only obvious difference is with our size and skin, or scales in the Krozan's case. We could have a few different organs and the Krozans, if I remember the picture Mr. Chittle showed us, don't have ears like ours."

"Unfortunately, none of that helps us solve our major problem. What are we supposed to do to help the Krozans?" Baya said.

"Mr. Chittle, what are we supposed to do next?" Drake asked.

"I do not know. Our instructions all along were to bring you here."

"Can you turn the main computer back on?" Baya asked.

"No," the chittle said.

"Who can help us now?" Baya asked.

"Only the Krozans," the chittle replied.

"How can they help us if they are all asleep in their hibernation tubes?" Baya asked.

Drake had an idea. "We'll have to wake one."

"How?" Baya asked.

"We cannot do that," Mr. Chittle said. "The process is dangerous and involves a number of steps. If not done right the Krozan will die."

"Can't you walk us through the steps?"Drake asked.

"No, I have tried to access the details from the command center computer, but because the process is automated I can only find the command that is given to bring everyone out of hibernation. That does not work because the link to the units is offline," the chittle said.

"Can we manually awaken them?" Drake asked.

"Of course. But if they are brought out of hibernation manually, a doctor has to treat the Krozans, or they will die," the chittle said.

"That's not good," Baya said.

"Except for Zane," the chittle said.

"What?" Drake said.

"Zane," the chittle said.

"Zane what?" Baya said.

"For some reason, the last communication the central computer had with me mentioned Zane. The name was not included in any command or information download," the chittle said.

"Mr. Chittle, didn't you think the name might be important?" Baya said.

"Not at the time," it said.

"Why is Zane different?" Drake asked.

"He had an accident when he was young and no longer has legs that function. As a result of the accident, Zane also has an artificial organ. It is this organ that doctors have to treat and monitor if a Krozan is awakened manually," the chittle said.

"So we can wake Zane up and he will survive?" Drake asked.

"Yes. It is very interesting that the central computer sent his name to me, and now you are talking about him."

"Seems obvious to me," Baya said to Drake. "Where can we find Zane?"

"Not far. Should we go there now?" the chittle asked.

"Yes," both Drake and Baya said at the same time.

"Follow me," the chittle said and slid across the floor and out the same door through which they had entered the room.

From there the three traveled down a short hallway before turning left and onto a hallway that went on as far as they could see. On both sides of the hall were doors about every twenty feet.

"Are these rooms where the Krozans live?" Drake asked.

"Yes," the chittle said. He stopped suddenly in front of a door to one of the rooms. "This is Zane's room."

While Drake didn't see a door knob, Baya saw a bump on the wall next to the door that looked similar to the bump she had observed and pushed to open the door that led in from the recreation area shortly after the two arrived on the ship. She pushed the bump, and the door to Zane's room opened.

CHAPTER 15

The first thing that struck Drake was the size of the bed. It took up nearly a third of the room. A desk that looked very similar to how the chittle looked when it demonstrated how it could become a desk was fastened to a nearby wall. A pile of metallic cubes and disks had been neatly piled next to the bed.

"That must be Zane," Baya said, referring to the figure on the bed.

"What is he wrapped in?" Drake asked.

"That is his hibernation tube. It seems to be functioning well," the chittle said.

"How can you tell?" Baya asked.

"The tube is connected to the control box on the wall next to the bed, and the light is still on. That light would be off if it was not working well," the chittle said.

Drake looked at a short tube that ran from a spot where Drake imagined Zane's shoulders were to the control box on the wall. The tube, like most everything else on the ship appeared to be made out of metal and was about an inch in diameter, not much different than the width of a garden hose, he thought.

"What's that smell in here?" Baya asked.

Drake had noticed it too. To him it smelled like one of his mother's air fresheners that she would spray in the air of a room if she thought it smelled bad.

"Since these rooms are sealed, they are constantly treated

with a spray that prevents germs and molds from developing. The Krozans like this odor," the chittle said.

"It's okay with me, too," Drake said. "Now, Mr. Chittle, what do we have to do to wake Zane without hurting him?"

"Move the switch on the control box to the spot where there are two stars," it said.

Drake walked over to the control box and studied it for a second. Right on the top of the box, he saw the switch. It looked easy to operate. Baya approached him and looked over his shoulder.

"How do you think he will react when he sees us?" she asked.

"Scared, mixed up, I would probably think I was dreaming."

"Are we dreaming right now?"

"No, I'm way past thinking that," Drake said. He looked back down at the lever, gripped it between his thumb and finger, and slid it from its position next a symbol with three stars to the one with two stars. The lever moved easily and clicked into position. The light on the box started flashing.

"The light is flashing on and off," Baya said.

"Good," the chittle responded. "Now we wait for the light to go off. When that happens you have to move the switch to the one star position."

"How long will that take?" Drake asked.

"As long as it does. My information only indicates that it varies with each Krozan. The science committee will be very interested in our results. I don't think anyone has ever been through this before," the chittle said.

"What? If it's never been done before, then why are we doing this?" Drake asked.

"You misunderstand me. Manually awakening someone has

been done many times before, but always in a laboratory setting and after a much shorter period of time," it said.

"How much shorter?" Baya asked.

"Almost two years shorter," the chittle said. "The laboratory experiments never had anyone in hibernation for over a month."

Baya and Drake looked at each other.

"This is crazy," Baya said, and Drake nodded.

"Quick, now, the light has gone out," the chittle said.

Drake slid the lever over to the one-star position, and the two teenagers looked over at Zane. At first nothing happened, but then they heard a crackling sound, and the wrap around Zane started to pull apart in a number of different areas. As it did, the wrap laid out flat on the bed. After about a minute, the entire wrap had come off Zane and lay flat on the bed under and around him.

They could see that Zane had worn a tight-fitting body suit that looked like it could have been made with something similar to Spandex. Drake saw a number of small holes in the suit.

"Is he okay?" Baya asked.

"Zane, are you awake?" Drake asked. Although Zane did not respond, Drake saw Zane's right hand twitch. "He moved."

"Then he should be fine," the chittle said. "Zane, we need you awake now."

Zane's right arm moved slightly, and a few seconds later, he moved his hand up to his eyes. He rubbed them much like a human would do while trying to wake up.

"Zane, wake up. We need your help," Baya said. Her voice must have surprised Zane because his eyes opened, and he tried to sit up before collapsing back on the bed.

"What? Who are you?" Zane asked.

"They are here to help us. Don't let their strange looks trouble you. They may be ugly, but they are here to help," the chittle said.

Zane sat up and stared at Drake and Baya. Despite what the chittle had said, Drake could sense fear coming from Zane.

"Your ship has been severely damaged, and we think you can help...."

"Status report," Zane said, interrupting Drake. The chittle slid next to Zane's bed, and its table top once again turned into a bright computer screen. Zane reached over and tapped the screen a few times. Each time he did a different screen appeared.

"This is terrible," Zane said. "Why did you select me to revive?" he asked while still studying the computer screen.

"You are the only Krozan who could live through a manual awakening without a doctor's assistance," the chittle said.

"Oh, yes, I remember that, but wasn't that only a theory?" Zane said.

"Yes, but as we have just learned, a good one," the chittle answered.

Drake noticed that Zane smiled at the chittle's answer. He remembered Baya's earlier remark when she said how similar she was to him and how the Krozans, other than their lizard like skin and features, were similar to them, too.

"We are very happy that you are awake, and we hope that you can help us figure out how we can fix the ship," Drake said.

"Why are you interested in fixing our ship?" Zane asked. He continued scrolling through the computer screens.

"It needs fixing before everyone dies," Baya said.

"Yes, I see, but why do you care? Who are you, and how did you get here?" Zane asked without looking up.

"It's a long story, and one that we don't fully understand

either. The one thing we do know is that we don't want to die on this ship, and the best chance for our survival is to help you stop this ship from falling apart," Drake said.

"I'm Baya and this is Drake, and to answer your other question, we're not really sure," Baya said.

Zane finally looked up. "This ship is drifting, everything has been shut down. Even the central computer is not functioning."

"We know that," Drake said. "We need a plan. Hopefully, you can come up with one, and the three of us can carry it out."

"Zane is at the head of his class. He will be able to lead us," the chittle said.

"There are too many systems down. I have no idea which one to try to fix first. Give me a prioritized list," Zane said.

At first, Drake thought Zane was talking to him, but then he realized it was a command for the chittle.

"There's a dozen items in the top category. It's impossible," Zane said after studying the list.

Drake could hear the frustration in his voice. "What is the top category?"

"Repairing the systems that keep the ship functioning. Without a fix to these, we will all die, and they all need immediate attention. Even if we knew how, it's too much for us," Zane said.

"If we had twenty more Krozans to help, could it be done?" Baya asked.

"Maybe, twice that many would be better, but that system is down," Zane said.

"Then, why don't we fix that system first?" Drake asked, understanding where Baya was leading to with her question.

"Yes, excellent idea," the chittle said. "If we can awaken the engineers, they may be able to fix the ship."

"But, we'd have to fix the broken link first," Zane said.

"Yes, that needs to be fixed," the chittle agreed.

"Oh, my, we have a warning that battery power is low," Zane said. "Are all the other power systems down?"

"Yes," the chittle said.

"I see that now, too. That changes everything, but what can we do? Wait a second. It says here there has been significant damage to the shuttle fleet and to their storage hangar, but the space shuttles have auxiliary power units that can generate power. Any reason we couldn't plug a few of them in the system to keep the batteries charged? Some of them must still work," Zane said.

"Excellent idea, Zane, but getting to them may be difficult," the chittle said.

"We have to try," Drake said.

Zane looked at Drake like he was seeing him for the first time. "I like your attitude, Drake," he said. "We need to go now, and while we are on the way there, you two must tell me how you got here and more about who you are."

"We'll certainly tell you all we know," Baya said.

Zane scooted off the side of the bed, and when he did something slid out with him from under the bed. Drake and Baya watched as the item opened into what looked like a wheel chair without the wheels.

"It's how I get around. My legs are useless." He tapped on a small panel built into the armrest. "This battery is fully charged. Let's go," Zane said and his chair floated out the door and into the hallway.

"That's cool," Drake said.

CHAPTER 16

*Z*ane scooted down the hall at such a fast pace that Drake and Baya had to jog after him. The chittle had no problem staying next to Zane.

"How does he expect for us to tell him about ourselves if we can't even keep up," Drake said.

Baya grinned at him and started to run a little faster. Drake moaned but ran faster, too. They slowed to a walk when they came to a section of the hallway where the wall to their left had been split open leaving a good view to a damaged section of the ship. Zane stared at the damage but didn't say anything. Once past the damaged wall, he sped up again.

They took a side corridor that led to a ramp that went down at a steep angle for about thirty yards into a large room.

"This is one of the ship's mechanical storage areas. Luckily it's not damaged, because the others are far from here," Zane said.

Drake thought they had run pretty far to get here, but didn't say anything. "What do we need?" he asked.

"From what I can tell, both the ship's main wireless system and the backup were destroyed by an explosion. The ship has a cable backup, but a few of those cables were cut affecting some of the communication links. One of those links connected the hibernation units to the command computer. I think we can repair that cable," Zane said.

"I thought we were going to supply power first," Baya asked.

"Yes, but it's been pointed out to me that if we returned power to that system first, repairing the cable would then be very dangerous, and since we have only two helpers, it would not be wise to lose one of you," Zane said.

Drake thought he again saw a little smile develop on Zane's face.

"Who pointed that out to you? Mr. Chittle?" Baya asked.

"Yes, but why do you call him by name?" Zane asked.

"It's a girl thing," Drake said, and this time he definitely saw a smile on Zane's face.

"I understand," Zane said, "we have girls, too."

"Funny, funny," Baya said. "Shouldn't we be hurrying?"

"Yes, we must hurry," the chittle agreed.

"Okay," Zane said. He reached out and grabbed a large bag made of what looked like tin foil and rested it on his lap. "This should be all we need if the cut cable isn't too bad."

"What is it?" Baya asked.

"A long length of cable that we should be able to use to connect the two ends of the broken cable together, and--"

A distant explosion shook the ship and interrupted Zane's answer. "And," he continued, "we better hurry."

Zane sped off and Baya and Drake were forced to race after him.

"If I remember right," Baya said, "you named Mr. Chittle."

Drake grinned and gave Baya a soft, playful punch to the shoulder.

Just about when Drake thought he would have to quit running, Zane stopped in front of a door.

"I think this is it," Zane said. He pushed the bump next to the door and it slid open. "Oh, I forgot the lights were out. Drake and

Baya stay close to me. Part of this tunnel might have been damaged."

Zane entered the tunnel and turned on a dim spotlight situated on the armrest of his chair. It cast barely enough light ahead of them to see in the darkness. The tunnel turned out to be a ramp about eight feet wide that spiraled downward at a fairly steep angle.

"We have a few of these tunnels throughout the ship to transport large equipment. Access panels to most of the ship's operating systems can also be found in the tunnels. We're just using this one to get to the eighty second level, since the elevators are not working and I can't use the ladders. Look out for that hole over there."

Drake couldn't see anything in the darkness. "I think we will be staying right behind you, so let us know if you go over any holes," Drake said.

"I need to avoid the holes, too, so that won't be a problem. My chair works off a magnetic field, so it doesn't operate over open air. It needs to be within a foot or two of the metal floor. If the floor disappeared under me, I would drop as fast as you would."

"That makes sense," Baya said. "I was wondering how it worked, and I do have another question. How does the ship make and maintain the artificial gravity?

"I don't know exactly. That's something I could study in college, if I wanted to, but what I do know is there are dozens of very large, spinning iron orbs positioned at various locations along the bottom of the ship. Each one produces a gravitational pull and combined they produce what you feel on this ship," Zane said.

Drake enjoyed science, but this was too technical to be

interesting to him. "Since your planet has been traveling in space for a long time, have you ever encountered other living beings in space?"

"Never, I'm still not sure if you two are real, or if I'm dreaming all this," Zane said.

"I stopped thinking we were dreaming when that large beam almost killed me," Baya said.

"Well, I stopped thinking we were dreaming some time ago, too," Drake said.

Zane led them off the ramp and out of the tunnel. A lot more evidence of the ship's damage surrounded them than in the prior hallways they'd been on.

They had to travel at a slow walk just to be safe. Large sections of the walls were cracked and even missing in some spots. The ceiling displayed gaping holes and even the floor of the hallway became dangerous in spots where basketball size holes could trip them if they didn't pay attention. Debris was everywhere.

"This is terrible," Zane said.

"This is minor," Drake said. "The ship has at least one huge section completely destroyed. We had to cross it on a single beam that isn't even there anymore. We barely made it across before it broke, too."

"We are here," the chittle said.

Zane stopped and looked around. He approached the edge of the hall at a point where a section of the wall had been damaged. A piece of the wall about the size of Drake's bedroom window was missing. This hole extended up from the floor.

"There," Zane said and moved to a point where he could reach out and grab a cable dangling from the side of the hole. He tugged at it and brought the end of the cable onto his lap where he studied it for a few seconds. He tore the aluminum foil bag and removed the extension cable. "This should work," he said and connected the extension cable to the broken end of the cable that he had pulled out to his lap. He held it up to show to Drake and Baya.

"Looks good," Baya said. "But what do we connect the other end of the extension cable to?"

Zane stuck his head through the gap in the wall and looked down. "Well, at least I can see the other end." He moved away from the hole on the wall, and both Baya and Drake bent down, leaned out, and looked down at the debris below them.

"It looks like whatever room was next to this one collapsed into the level below, or maybe two levels collapsed. Is that the cable dangling over there?" Drake asked pointing at a length of cable that hung almost to the debris pile below them.

"I believe so, but I have no idea how we can get to it," Zane said.

"At our past traveling speed, it will take about thirty minutes to reach the entrance to that area, and the damage has most likely jammed that doorway," the chittle said. "My power will have run out by then."

"Well, Mr. Chittle, we can't have that," Baya said and jumped through the gap in the wall.

"Baya!" both Drake and Zane said at the same time.

Drake leaned through the gap in the wall and looked for Baya.

"Why did she do that? Is she okay?" Zane asked.

"She's fine and almost to the cable. She landed on a chunk of metal that's sticking out from the wall below us and is using other spots along the wall to hang onto. Be careful, Baya!" Drake shouted to her.

"That's impressive," Zane said. He moved in close to Drake and leaned out. They both watched as she made her way back toward them carrying the end of the cable in one hand. "That must be hard."

"A little," Baya said, balancing on a small crack in the wall below and to the left of them while reaching up with her free hand to find another spot to grab. In a few seconds, she was only a yard away when the cable wouldn't get any closer. "It must have either lost a section or is caught somewhere."

"That's okay, we have plenty of extension cable," Zane said. He swung the free end of the extension cable to her.

She tried to grab it with the same hand that she held the other end of the cable with, but was unsuccessful. "I can't let go with my other hand, or I'll fall."

"Stay there," Drake said. He lay on his stomach and slid out as far as he felt safe and reached for the cable. Baya gave it to him, and with his other hand, he took the extension cable from Zane. "Now how does this fasten together?"

"Bring the two ends together. Once in contact, they should bond automatically," Zane said and watched as Drake pushed them together. "That bond is fragile so you'll need to pull the outer layer of the extension cable over the original cable. Just wrap your hand around it pull it over."

Drake did as he was told and was impressed at how easy everything was. "I think it's done," he said.

"Okay, let's go find some power," Zane said.

Drake pushed himself back from the ledge and then helped Baya climb through. After they were both standing, Drake realized he was still holding her hand. Embarrassed, he let go.

"I didn't mind," Baya whispered.

"Come along, you two, keep up," Zane said.

"At least we're getting our exercise," Drake said to Baya.

She grinned and nodded her head. The two raced after Zane for five minutes before Zane slowed to a stop next to an open room that was filled with large equipment.

"Is this the shuttle bay?" Drake asked, breathing hard.

"No, that's way below us. This is where we'll pick up our ride to get us there," Zane said and moved toward what looked like a giant bowling ball. "Now, all we have to do is open that door."

"What is this?" Drake couldn't see a door on the ball. It towered over him, and the surface of the ball appeared smooth with the exception of three holes that were about a foot deep before being sealed by metal plates. He guessed the ball was about fifteen feet in diameter.

"It's a repair and inspection vehicle. It can be used inside or outside the ship. Drake could you lift Baya up, so she can open the door," Zane asked.

"Yes," Drake said, "but where is the door."

"It's right in front of us, but you can only see the bump where the opener is," Zane said.

Drake studied the side of the ball and finally spotted the round bump. He walked closer to the ball and jumped while stretching out his arm in an effort to reach the opener. He came close to it, but it was too high.

"Pick me up," Baya said.

Drake considered the options and finally hooked his two hands together and instructed Baya to step into his hands. She did, and he stood up, lifting her foot to his waist. She kept her balance and reached up. Her fingers just reached the bump.

"Swoosh," a door directly in front of Drake opened in a flash and almost made him lose his balance. Baya jumped down, and the pair looked inside the ball. Lights went on and a soft humming sound could be heard.

"Good, everything seems to be in order. I was worried the batteries might not work after being off for so long. Let's get inside," Zane said.

The door opened all the way to the floor of the ship's deck, and from inside, a ramp slid out leading up about four feet to a solid floor inside the repair vehicle.

"Can we all fit in here," Baya asked as she was the last one in.

"Yes, you two take those chairs," Zane said. He moved next to the wall and pulled a lever. A panel on the wall lit up and slid down to a point right in front of him. He pressed against the screen and two things happened.

First, the walls of the ship became transparent. Everywhere Drake looked, other than at the floor, was like looking out a clear window. Then, only a second or two later, the vehicle rose about two feet into the air and started gliding toward an opening at the far end of the room. When they reached it, Drake saw that the opening led to a short-curved tunnel that took them into a large open space.

The vehicle floated out into the air and slowly descended toward a dozen or so space shuttles that didn't look much different than the ones he had seen on the television show Star Trek or in the Star Wars movies.

"Looks like only the emergency lighting is on. Let's hope their battery packs last as long as we're in here. This large room is our shuttle bay. See all the cranes protruding from the wall? We use those with the larger transport ships that are attached to the outer hull," Zane said.

Drake saw signs of significant damage along the wall on one side of the shuttle bay. "At least there are no fires," he said.

"Fires shouldn't be a worry. We have mobile repair units that are very good at putting out any fires," Zane said.

"There were seventy-four fires on the ship at my last update, but that was a while ago, and I am no longer receiving any updates," the chittle said.

Drake had not noticed the chittle coming on board the repair vehicle. Having it still with them was reassuring.

"Fires, still? That's horrible," Zane said. "I am still having a hard time accepting all this. I don't know what is harder to believe, that I've been in hibernation for two years or that you two are really here. Are you two mates?"

"What?" Drake asked.

"Your face is turning red. Does that mean something?" Baya asked grinning.

Embarrassed, Drake didn't respond right away.

"No, but why do you ask?" Baya said.

"I sense a very strong bond between the two of you," Zane said. "You look like you belong together."

"I sense that too," Baya said and again grinned at Drake.

Girls, Drake thought, why do they tease so much? But, at the same time, he knew he felt the same as Baya.

"Good," Zane said, and at first, Drake thought he was talking about the two of them again. "While there has been damage to some of the shuttles, all the power units look okay."

"Are those small boxes the power units?" Drake asked.

"Yes. We'll need to get two, better yet three units. We can connect them in series to the ship's power grid. That should do it," Zane said.

"Can just three of those things can power the entire ship?" Baya asked.

"Oh no, we'll only use this power to restore internal communications and the command center computer. Once it responds, we'll shut down everything else. If we correctly repaired the communications link to the hibernation control hub, the command computer can start the automated awakening process," Zane said.

"Sounds like a good plan," Drake said.

"If we succeed, I'm pretty confident the engineers can get the ship working again," Zane said.

"We'll succeed, but I suggest we don't wake too many of your shipmates until the power is restored," Baya said.

"She's right. Life support systems have already been shut down in many parts of the ship and remaining battery power is at critical. The power units we will be using won't last long either," the chittle said.

"Well then, let's get to it," Zane said and landed the craft next to the cluster of power units.

CHAPTER 17

They left the repair vehicle and hurried to the nearest power unit.

"This looks good," Zane said. "Let's push it over to that spot on the wall." He pointed to a spot on a nearby wall.

Drake tried to push the power unit, but it didn't budge.

"Wait a second," Zane said and, approaching the unit, pulled down a small lever that stuck out from a side panel. The power unit instantly lifted a foot off the floor. "Now try it."

Drake pushed and the unit floated in the direction of the wall. He hurried after it and continued gently pushing it. In a few seconds, he realized he would have to stop it or it would bump into the wall. He grabbed a section of the frame where he could get a grip and was surprised how easily it stopped. Impressed with himself, he looked back and saw Zane gliding toward him with one by his side. Next to him he saw Baya walking with a power unit next to her.

"That was easy," Drake said when they were all together.

"We haven't done anything yet. Let's hook these up. Baya pull that cap off and bring the cable over here," Zane pointed at the power unit next to Baya.

"This one?" Baya asked and reached for a round thing that looked like the plastic lid to a large peanut butter jar, except this one was made out of metal.

"Yes, just pull it straight off."

She did and the end of a cable popped out a few inches. She grabbed it and pulled it to Zane. He took it from her and stuck the end of the cable into a small opening in the side of the power unit he had next to him.

"Drake, your turn," Zane said and pointed to Drake's power unit.

Drake had already located the cable on his unit and pulled it to Zane, who stuck the end of the cable into a second small opening next to the one he had just filled with the cable from Baya's unit. Next, Zane scooted around the power unit next to him, pulled its cable out, and pressed the end into an opening on the wall.

"This should work," Zane said. "He touched the screen on the table top of the chittle. Make sure the command computer knows to immediately shut the power off to everything but the hibernation units and life support in that area only. Keep the communications link up, too."

"So this power will wake up the main computer?" Baya asked.

"Yes, but the other systems on the ship may also try to draw on the power. It is essential that everything else is shut off or these units may overload and shut down. That would be disastrous," Zane said.

"The command center computer will know your instructions as soon as it starts. I will monitor everything. You know life support to this area will shut off, too," the chittle said.

"Yes," Zane said, "but this is a very large area, so we'll be fine for a long time. You included the ship's captain and senior staff along with the engineers, right?"

"Of course," the chittle responded, "just as you instructed.

The engineers can start working repairs, and the senior staff can prioritize how to best proceed with the others. That is protocol and would have happened long ago if the communications links weren't destroyed."

"Right," Zane said. "Unfortunately, we are now doing this at the very last moment. Let's hope it works." He reached over to the unit next to him and punched a spot on the side of it.

A soft humming began. At first, just from the unit he touched, but within seconds the other two units started humming. Panels of blue and green lights turned on and a screen lit up on each. Zane dragged a finger across the screen on the unit next to him. The humming became a little louder.

"It's working," the chittle said.

"Hurry," Zane said. He stared at his unit's computer screen. "Come on, hang in there, just a little longer."

The unit next to Drake started vibrating. He stepped away from it and looked over at Baya. Her unit seemed fine, and she had her eyes fixed on Zane.

"I don't know," Zane said and started shaking his head.

Suddenly, the humming decreased, and Drake's unit stopped vibrating.

"Did it not work?" Drake asked. He stepped over and took Baya's hand in his. She squeezed his hand.

Zane and the chittle remained silent.

Drake wanted to ask the question again, but before he could Zane finally answered him.

"So far, so good" he said.

"The command center computer is functioning and understands our instructions," the chittle said.

"Fantastic!" Drake said.

"How long will it take for them to wake up?" Baya asked.

"Only a few minutes," Zane said.

"How will they know what's going on?" Drake asked.

"There is a protocol for them to follow, and as part of that protocol they will first check on the ship's status and any tasks they have been assigned," the chittle said. "If I may say so, I think they will be shocked by what they will read."

"Is that what you were doing when you first woke up," Drake asked Zane.

"Yes, but I had the added benefit of you two being there," Zane said. "Explain again how we got into this predicament. I know about the collision with the radiation stream, but what happened after that."

Drake thought he was being asked the question and started to say he wasn't too straight on that either when the chittle spoke.

"It's rather straight forward, but unfortunate. As a direct consequence of the initial series of explosions, poisonous gases spread throughout the ship faster than the ship could filter them. Four Krozans died before the senior staff decided that the hibernation process was the safest way to protect everyone. By the time the air quality had improved, subsequent explosions and fires had damaged the communication cables and the wireless system on the ship. The command center computer couldn't get the order to awaken everyone to the hibernation consoles," the chittle explained.

"But doesn't protocol call for two officers to remain on the bridge? Why couldn't they do it?" Zane asked.

"Those two died," the chittle said.

"Oh, too bad. This has to be the worst disaster in history," Zane said.

"And, if it wasn't for the arrival of Drake and Baya, it would have been a lot worse," the chittle said.

"We owe you our highest appreciation," Zane said. "I'll recommend that you both receive our world's highest medal for bravery."

"Thank you," Baya said, "but I don't feel very brave."

"Captain Brail is now awake and is communicating with the command center computer. I think our plan is working," the chittle said.

"Good," Drake said. "You know, Zane, Mr. Chittle here and the rest of the chittles played a major role in all this. We never could have done anything without their help."

"They are rather fantastic," Baya said.

"Yes, but they are only machines," Zane said.

"You have become accustomed to them. We don't have machines on our worlds that are so advanced. At least to me, they are more than just a machine," Drake said.

"Maybe so," Zane said. "I have always liked them, but how do we reward them, other than saying thank you?"

"Excuse me," Mr. Chittle interrupted them. "Captain Brail has approved our plan and is now on his way to the command center. He has ordered the senior staff meet him there, and he has requested our presence."

CHAPTER 18

"*D*oes he know we are here?" Baya asked.

"He knows two aliens arrived on the ship and have helped in the rescue. He also knows Zane has helped," the chittle said.

"These power units will continue operating until their batteries run out. By then the engineers should have started repairs. We should head to the command center," Drake said.

"All the engineers and senior staff successfully came out of hibernation," the chittle said. "I'm going to try to get a quick recharge now," it said and slid up against the first power unit.

"Sounds like it's all done now except the waiting," Drake said.

"Yes, is there anything you'd like to ask of me?" Zane said.

"How did you get selected for this trip?" Baya asked.

"My parents volunteered to help colonize our new world, as did thousands of others. They were selected and as expected, brought me along."

"It will be a long time before people on our world will be able to leave our solar system. I doubt if I'll ever see a different world," Baya said.

"You've seen this spaceship, me and Zane, and don't forget Mr. Chittle. That has to be something," Drake said.

"Especially Mr. Chittle," Baya said.

"Ha!" Drake said.

Zane started to say something when a nearby explosion shook the shuttle bay. Drake almost fell down. A loud pop followed the explosion, and a small section of the giant doors that led from the shuttle bay to outer space broke and swung outward.

An alarm sounded, and Zane shouted, "Quick! Back to the repair vehicle!" Without waiting he glided away with the chittle by his side.

Drake grabbed Baya's hand and they both started running. Luckily they had left the door to the repair vehicle open. Baya and Drake raced into the vehicle seconds behind Zane, who closed the doors as soon as everyone was inside.

"What happened? Drake asked.

"That last explosion must have damaged the outer hull of the ship near here and somehow caused enough stress on the doors that the corner of that one bent open. In less than a minute, there won't be enough air in the whole shuttle bay for us to breathe. We're safe in here," Zane said.

"I guess we're lucky it's a big room and not a very large hole," Baya said.

"Yes we are. Did the inner doors seal?" Zane asked.

Drake looked out the window to see if he could tell.

"Yes, we may be stuck here for some time," the chittle said.

Drake grinned and wondered how long it would take him to get used to having Mr. Chittle around.

"Mr. Chittle, you and your friends should get a medal for your role in rescuing the ship," Drake said.

"I doubt that will happen," Zane said.

"What would you like to happen, Mr. Chittle?" Baya asked.

"I hope the ship gets fixed and that everyone will be fine," the chittle said. "Captain Brail is aware of our situation and will make rescuing us a priority. He is most interested in meeting both of you."

"What will happen to us?" Drake asked.

"I don't think we can get you back home," Zane said. "You'll be safe with us."

"We do have a problem," the chittle said.

"What now?" Zane asked.

"The command center computer now gives us a ninety five percent chance of saving this ship and then reaching our destination, but it will take time."

"That sounds good. So, what is the problem?" Zane asked.

"Our being rescued before our available air runs out."

"What do you mean?" Baya asked.

"The engineers and senior staff are busy trying to fix the ship. The priorities of those repairs do not include the damage to the shuttle bay door, and until that is sealed and the shuttle bay is re-pressurized, the interior doors will remain sealed," the chittle said.

"It may be uncomfortable, but why can't we wait in here?" Zane asked.

"This vehicle is not designed to operate for long periods of time outside the spaceship," the chittle said.

"But it's producing oxygen isn't it? I mean, I feel like I'm breathing fresh air," Drake said.

"Yes, it has a limited ability to operate outside the ship," the chittle said. "In our case we may still be inside the ship, but with the hole created by the damaged door, all the air has been sucked out of the shuttle bay. It's just like being out there."

"How long do we have?" Zane asked.

"Eight hours," the chittle replied.

"Then we simply have to solve the problem ourselves," Baya said.

Drake nodded. "What options do we have, Mr. Chittle?"

"We could fix the door, but we would need heavier equipment, so I don't believe that is a possibility. The better option is to try to get outside the shuttle bay and come in a different entrance."

"That sounds like a plan," Drake said.

"I've never flown any type ship or vehicle in space before," Zane said. "We have gravity inside the ship, but out there, we won't."

"You just have to be really gentle on the thrusters," Drake said.

"I thought you said you've never been on a spaceship," Zane said.

"That's true, but I have a video game that plays like a space shuttle simulator. It's supposed to be realistic," Drake said somewhat embarrassed.

"Then you may have to pilot this vehicle," Zane said.

"But," Drake started to say something, but Baya took his arm in her hand.

"Zane is correct. You should fly this vehicle once we are out of this ship," she said. "If you have practiced something similar, you have the advantage over the two of us."

"It is only a matter of direction and velocity," the chittle said.

"Can you do it, Mr. Chittle?" Drake asked.

"No. These vehicles have to be flown by a Krozan, or I suppose, by an Earthling," the chittle said. "I can advise you if you're doing it correctly or not."

"A back-seat driver, Mr. Chittle?" Drake asked with a grin.

"Why yes, that's what I'll be," the chittle replied not understanding the joke.

"Hush," Baya said and gently punched Drake in the arm. "He may not have understood that, but I did."

Zane said something to the chittle, and the vehicle floated up in the air and toward the damaged door.

"Drake come here and watch these levers." Zane pointed to the panel to his left. "They move when I move mine. You'll be able to see how the instruments make the vehicle move around."

Drake moved to a spot next to Zane. Baya moved close behind Drake to look over his shoulder.

"Too bad we can't simply repair the door," Baya said.

"The door is too thick for us to fix, but we should be able to get the door to open a little," Zane said.

"Even with the power cut to this section of the ship?" Baya asked.

"Most everything on this ship has its own battery backup power source for emergencies, including the one we're in" Zane said.

"Much will be learned from this experience," Mr. Chittle said. "The command center computer has been documenting everything. It's very proud of its large data storage."

"You almost sound bitter, Mr. Chittle," Baya said.

"I am not programmed to be bitter, but we do get tired of it reminding us how much more important it is than the rest of us," the chittle said.

Drake watched as one lever on the panel in front of him moved to the right, and as it did, the repair vehicle floated right. When the lever moved back to the center, the vehicle stopped. He quickly learned how the levers affected the flight of the vehicle.

Three separate levers controlled how the vehicle maneuvered. The lever on the left controlled the speed. The one in the center controlled movements to the right, left, backwards and forward. The one on the right moved the vehicle up and down. The vehicle never moved very fast, and Drake didn't think it would be very hard to fly. He did wonder how much more difficult it would be to control outside the ship, and why Zane didn't want to pilot the vehicle once out in space.

"Baya, go back to the seat you were in. I need you to operate the extension arm to open the door," Zane said.

Baya returned to her seat.

"Find the red lever," Zane said. "Turn the knob at the top to the right and then push the lever upward. You should see the extension arm. It has a clasp at the end of it, but we won't be using the clasp."

Baya watched as a silver pole extended out about fifteen feet from the vehicle. "It's out," she said.

"I'm going to move us right next to the pad that controls the door. When we get there, you'll need to press the green pad and then get ready to press the red pad when I tell you to," Zane said.

"How do I do that?" Baya asked.

"You can move the arm back in towards us by pushing the lever down. You can stop its movement by putting it back in the center position. You can also move it right or left the same way by moving the lever to the right or left. Each time you want to stop its movement, put the lever in that center position. Right now, I suggest you bring the arm back in about a foot. That will allow you to extend it into the pad when we're in the right spot," Zane said.

Baya played with the lever, and by the time they reached the cluster of lights and panels next to the door, she felt she knew how to use the extension arm.

"Okay, see if you can push the green pad for about three seconds, and then be ready to push on the red one," Zane said.

Baya had no trouble pressing the end of the extension against the green pad.

The large doors slowly slid open.

"Press the red one now. One press should do it," Zane said.

Baya moved the arm to the left about one foot to a spot in front of the red pad. She pushed the lever up and the arm extended until it made contact with the red pad.

The shuttle bay doors stopped moving.

"Captain Brail wants to know what we are doing. He has noted that we have opened the bay doors," the chittle said.

"I guess it's time we told him," Zane said.

"I did," the chittle said. "He thinks our chances are better if we stay in the ship. No, I should correct that. He thinks we have no chance if we leave the safety of the ship."

"What do you think, Zane?" Drake asked.

"I think we have eight hours either way," Zane said. "They have less time than that to get the ship's power back up and to reawaken the rest of the Krozans on board. Their priority has to be that. Repairing the shuttle bay doors or overriding the safeguards by opening an interior door for us would require too much time and a work crew they don't have right now or couldn't spare if they did."

"Then we need to try to save ourselves," Baya said.

"Let's do it," Drake said.

Zane flew the small vehicle toward the opening to outer space.

CHAPTER 19

As soon as the vehicle floated out the door two things happened. Everything outside became very dark and the vehicle began to tumble. Baya turned to look at Zane and Drake and suddenly found herself floating.

"Better hold onto something," Zane said. "I'm safe because my chair is secured to the floor."

Drake grabbed the side of the counter, but before he could brace his feet, his legs started floating up behind him. "Wow!" he said. "This is cool."

"You need to brace yourself with your feet under something so you can stand here and fly this thing," Zane said. "I'll try to stop the repair vehicle from tumbling."

At first, Zane's efforts appeared to only make things worse. The tumbling didn't affect Drake as in space there is no up and down, and the ship's movements didn't cause him to fall one way or the other. However, Drake knew if he was going to fly the vehicle to any point on the massive space ship they just left, he needed the repair vehicle to be stable.

Every time Zane tried to stop the vehicle from tumbling in one direction, he just caused it to tumble in a different one.

"Let me try," Drake said. This was just like in his favorite video game where he had to dock a space shuttle with the space station. The game was based on actual procedures used by NASA pilots and simulated flying in outer space.

His video game used a joy stick, so using the three levers on the panel in front of him made flying the repair vehicle a little more difficult, but in no time he had them stable and flying alongside the big ship.

"Fantastic!" Baya shouted.

"Very good," Zane said.

Even Drake wondered how he had mastered the controls so quickly. Could the magic from the coin still be helping him? He hoped so. "Where do we go?"

"Might I suggest the recovery bay? It's large enough to accommodate us and not too far from here," the chittle said.

"Good choice," Zane said.

"How do we get there?" Drake said.

"Fly, of course," Zane said, "but if you mean where is it, I have it marked on the screen up here."

Drake looked up at a large computer screen that displayed a picture of the ship with a spot of red marking the recovery bay. The repair vehicle's location was displayed by a small picture of the vehicle.

"Thanks," Drake said. He looked out the window and started flying toward the front of the ship. To be safe, he kept the repair vehicle forty yards away from the space ship. Despite the darkness, they could see the space ship quite clearly.

"I can't get over how big your ship is, Zane," Baya said.

"It's the largest space ship we have. Look at that," he said and pointed to a large crack in the ship's hull. "It's amazing the ship held together. I don't think they will be able to fix that until we get to a spaceport."

"Fortunately, the ship can make the remainder of the trip without the systems damaged and sealed off by that crack. The command center computer has reported that the engineers have already shut off the fuel generation systems. That will make fire fighting a lot easier, and once the fires are out, the threat of more explosions should be over," the chittle said.

"Good," Baya said.

"There's the recovery bay over there," Zane said and pointed to a spot ahead of them.

Drake steered them toward it and started to slow them down.

"Baya, get ready to work the extension arm again," Zane said. "This time it will be a little bit harder. There are two steps to opening the bay doors from the outside."

Baya had already returned to her chair. "I'm ready."

"Drake can you bring us close to that panel," he pointed to a large black panel on the side of the ship. The lights from the repair vehicle provided enough light for Baya to clearly see the panel.

"I'll try," Drake said and worked the levers to slowly move the repair vehicle close to the panel.

"Baya, press the panel near the bottom left corner. You just need to press it once," Zane said.

Baya extended the arm and pressed the panel. A yellow light lit up the entire panel, but nothing else happened.

"Now we have to wait for the light to turn red," Zane said. "That will indicate everything is sealed off inside the ship and the doors will unlock."

"How long will that take?" Drake said.

"About twenty minutes," the chittle said.

"That's not too long to wait," Baya said. "Zane, are your parents on this ship?"

"Yes they are, and my little sister is with us."

"They'll certainly be proud of you for rescuing everyone," Baya said.

"I've done very little," Zane said. "You two saved us."

"No, we really did nothing but wake you," Baya said.

"But, if you hadn't done that, we would have all died," Zane said.

"Zane is correct," the chittle said. "You had to overcome many challenges and almost died trying to help us. The three of you will always be remembered as heroes."

"We have already discussed this," Drake said. "I think we should hold off on anymore hero talk until we're safe inside, and the Krozans are safely on their way to their new home."

Zane thought for a second before speaking. "You're right. There are still more challenges ahead, but I'm going to recommend that you two get a top floor apartment to live in once we reach our destination."

"A top floor apartment? Together?" Drake asked.

"Yes. The top floor apartments are everyone's favorite because they provide the best views. Usually only the leaders and others with influence get the top floor. I think you two deserve to live together in our best apartments," Zane said.

"Thank you," Baya said, grinning at Drake who was already starting to blush. "I wonder if our children will be blue."

Drake didn't know what to say. He knew Baya was teasing him again, but he still couldn't think of a good response.

"How about you, Mr. Chittle? I don't think you ever gave me an answer before. What would you like as a reward?" Baya asked.

"What you would give me would be given to all the chittles. We are many, but we are also one," the chittle said.

"That might make it hard," Zane said.

"Not really, we would like a name," the chittle said.

"A name," Baya said with a big smile, "that's a great idea."

"But wouldn't every chittle have to have a different name?" Drake asked.

"No, we don't have a name now, but we always know when someone is talking to us," the chittle said.

Baya said, "It makes sense to me. What name?"

"Mister Chittle," it said.

"Awesome," Drake said.

"I think you actually first gave him that name," Baya said.

"Yes, you did, Drake, and I thank you," Mr. Chittle said.

"I'm not sure," Zane said.

"Oh, come on," Baya said.

They all laughed, even Zane whose laughter sounded strange.

Twenty minutes passed and then another twenty, but the light on the panel never changed colors.

"I believe there has been some damage inside the bay which is preventing the interior doors from closing and sealing off the recovery bay from the rest of the ship. If they can't close, this outer door cannot open," Mr. Chittle said.

"That's not good," Zane said.

"There is one other recovery bay that we could go to that might work, but the section of the ship where that bay is located has had its life support system shut down for a long time as part of the early power saving efforts after the collision," Mr. Chittle said.

"Then we can't go there," Zane said. "Isn't there a third recovery bay somewhere?"

"Yes, but that one was located where the large crack in the

ship's outer hull now exists," Mr. Chittle said. "It is no longer there."

"I hope we aren't out of options," Baya said.

"Didn't you say there are large shuttle craft attached to the outside of this spaceship?" Drake asked.

"Yes, there are four large shuttle craft that carry Krozans back and forth to our planet from the ship," Mr. Chittle said.

"Couldn't we get into one of those?" Drake asked.

"Yes, it might work," Zane said. Drake could hear the excitement in his voice.

"One of the four is damaged beyond repair, and one received some minor damage, but two of the shuttles were not damaged. They have their own life support systems and have cargo bays that can easily handle a repair vehicle of this size," Mr. Chittle said.

"Let's go there," Baya said.

"What direction do we take?" Drake asked. He started moving their small repair vehicle away from the spaceship.

"See that long section of the ship that points out to the right," Zane said pointing straight ahead of them.

"Yes."

"Go straight toward it. The shuttle craft we want is just next to it."

Drake started flying the vehicle toward the shuttle. "Why do you call the large bay we were first in the shuttle bay if the shuttle's are kept out here?"

"The regular size shuttle craft are kept there. The large ones like the one we are going to now are too large to fit inside. With a spaceship this size, we need the largest shuttles the fleet has," Zane said.

"That makes sense," Baya said. "Should we have gotten into one of the smaller ones back in the shuttle bay where we were?"

"It wasn't possible. We weren't near one when the large bay doors broke open. We barely made it back to this vehicle," Zane said.

"Zane is correct, and the shuttles back there are not big enough to let us fly this into them. The large shuttles will let us fly in and still have plenty of room to close its doors once we're inside. We must not delay. It will take time for the large shuttle to bring life support conditions to adequate levels," Mr. Chittle said.

"I believe we are approaching the shuttle now," Zane said.

"I can't see it," Drake said.

"It blends in with the ship," Zane said. "I highlighted it on the screen."

Drake looked up at the computer screen and saw the outline of the shuttle. He looked back down out the window, and now that he knew what to look for, he saw the outline of the large shuttle. "That is big."

"Yes, it can hold four hundred passengers plus their luggage," Zane said. "Bring us down next to the ship right there."

Again, Zane pointed to a spot on the ship, and Drake flew them toward the general area.

"A little more to the right," Zane gestured with his hand. "Good, good, right here."

Drake looked out the window and saw a panel on the side of the shuttle that looked very similar to the one on the spaceship.

"Baya, it's the same process. "Push the lower left corner."

Baya was already extending the arm toward the panel. She pushed it, and a yellow light lit up.

"We shouldn't have to wait as long for this one to get ready," Zane said.

Sure enough, barely a minute later, the light turned red.

"Good," Zane said. "Push the panel again."

Baya did and a circular opening in the side of the shuttle slowly opened.

"Let's get inside," Zane said, and Drake flew them into the shuttle craft.

"I've made contact with the shuttle's command computer. The doors should be closing behind us," Mr. Chittle said. "Life support systems have been turned back on, but it will be a while before we can leave this vehicle."

The outer doors are closed," Baya said. "Other than the light from us, it's pitch black in here." As soon as she said this, several lights turned on and lit up the room around them. "Thanks, Mr. Chittle, I'm assuming that was your doing."

"Yes, all systems are in working order on this ship. I have established contact with the main command center computer via this shuttle's computer system. The Captain has been informed of our status. He has instructed us to stay here."

Zane had already taken over the flying and had landed the vehicle. "Like we have any place else to go," he said. "We're lucky to be here."

Drake felt the artificial gravity from the large spaceship. "It feels good to sense what's up and down again."

"Yes," Baya said as she stood up, stretched and moved next to Drake. She took his hand in hers.

"I do have some bad news," Mr. Chittle said.

"What now?" Zane asked.

CHAPTER 20

"*B*y my calculations, we will run out of breathable air eight minutes before it will be safe to leave this recovery vehicle," Mr. Chittle said.

"That doesn't sound good," Drake said.

"We can conserve the air by sleeping," Zane said.

"Who can sleep now?" Baya said. "It's all I can do to just try to relax. But I will try."

"And I'm not exactly tired, having just slept for two years," Zane said.

"I don't see a place where we can lie down either," Drake said.

Baya studied the inside of the little vehicle and said, "You and I can sit down over here. The curve of the wall will let us at least lean backwards against it."

Drake knew she was talking to him. He watched her move over to the narrow spot between the various panels and equipment that lined the inside wall. She sat down, leaned back, and looked up at him.

"Are you sure there's room?" he asked.

"Yes. This is no time to be shy," Baya said.

He smiled at her and knew she was right. They might run out of oxygen soon. So any awkwardness he felt at the moment seemed silly. He squeezed into the small space next to her. She snuggled closer to him, and he had little choice but to put his arm around her shoulders. She rested her head on his shoulder.

"I wonder why I'm not more afraid right now," she said.

"That's a good point. I don't really feel afraid either. Think it's the magic coins?" he asked.

"You mean it's not me?" Baya teased.

"Or me?" Drake replied.

They both laughed.

"I think we'll last the extra eight minutes," Baya said. "Even if we don't sleep, we can relax and slow our breathing a little."

Drake looked over at Zane. "Is he sleeping?"

"Yes, the Krozans can make themselves fall asleep at will. Can't you two?" Mr. Chittle said.

"No," they both said at the same time.

"That is too bad; there may not be enough time. I have chronicled everything. You two will always be remembered by the Krozans," Mr. Chittle said.

"We'll be fine," Drake said.

He looked at Baya who smiled and closed her eyes. He closed his eyes and tried to sleep, but after ten or fifteen minutes he knew there was no chance that he would fall asleep.

"If we don't get to go home, besides missing our families, what would be the worst part for you?" Baya asked.

"The food here. How about you? What would be the worst part for you, and don't say being stuck with me."

"Oh, Drake, don't be silly. Being stuck with you would be the best part." She lifted her head off his shoulder and looked around the inside of the repair vehicle. "The food would be the worst part for me, too. I'm also worried about how we could get new clothes."

Drake chuckled. "I haven't thought about that."

"If we do get to go home, I'll really miss you," Baya said.

"I'd miss you, too, a whole bunch." Drake closed his eyes, wondering for the first time if he'd rather stay with Baya than go home.

"I'm feeling a little dizzy," Baya said.

"Me too. Maybe the air is starting to go bad," Drake said. He turned his head to look at Baya and was shocked. She had disappeared.

"Baya!" he shouted. A bright light flashed in front of him. "Baya!"

"Drake, what are you shouting about? People are staring." Drake saw his mother standing close by. He glanced around and saw that he was back in Disney World. The water in the small fountain appeared to still be rippling from the impact of the coin. "Are you okay?" his mother asked.

"But mom, how long have I been gone?" Drake asked.

"Gone? You haven't gone anywhere," she said. "And why were you shouting Baya? Is that someone's name?"

"Yes, it is," he said.

"Well, come on," his mother took him by the arm. "Your father has already located a place to get ice cream. He wants us to join him."

Drake walked with his mother, happy that he could lean against her a little for support. His mind was still trying to grasp what had just happened. It couldn't have been a dream, or had it? It seemed so real.

"Drake, is this some girl's hair on your shoulder?" his mother stopped and pulled two strands of hair off his shirt. "Why this is blue. I don't know why young girls these days dye their hair all these strange colors. Drake, I didn't know you had a girlfriend." She smiled in a way that Drake knew she was teasing him.

"There are a few things you don't know about me, Mom," Drake said. His mind cleared up. It hadn't been a dream. Baya was real, and he had been on that spaceship. The magic coin was real.

"Is she pretty?" his mother asked.

"Beautiful," Drake said.

"You'll have to introduce me to her."

"Hopefully, some day I can," Drake said, and he really meant it. He looked down at his tennis shoe and saw where the hot sealant from the beam slightly singed it.

He hoped Zane was okay and that Baya was home, too. He wondered if she was thinking of him.

CHAPTER 21

"Zane, you can wake up now. It's safe now to leave this vehicle," the chittle said.

"So we made it after all," Zane said opening his eyes.

"Yes, and you'll have no trouble staying on the shuttle until the crew can get things back to normal on the ship."

"Hey, where are Drake and Baya? Did they already get off?" Zane asked.

The door to the repair vehicle opened. "No, Zane, they vanished about thirty minutes ago. I think they went back to wherever they came from."

"Were they really here?" Zane asked.

"Yes. I double checked all my records and scans. They were here."

"Well, Mr. Chittle, I guess we can handle it from here," Zane said.

"Zane, that's the first time you called me Mr. Chittle."

"That is your name, isn't it?"

"Yes, it is," Mr. Chittle replied and while there might be no way of seeing it, Mr. Chittle was smiling.

THE END

Title: The Enchanted Coin

- Author: Bob Doerr
- Publisher: TotalRecall Publications, Inc.
- Paper Back: ISBN: 978-1-59095-084-5
- eBook: ISBN: 978-1-59095-085-2
- Audio ISBN: 978-1-59095-280-1
- Number of pages in the finished book: 130
- Publication Date: September 17, 2013

We have all heard of tales of UFO's, ghosts, people who say they can talk to the spirits, ancient curses, and magical talismans. Most of us automatically dismiss them as false, figments of people's imagination, and understandably so. However, might not just a few of them be true? I don't know, but I heard this story from a young man the other day who swore the fascinating tale I have set forth in this book really did really occur, because it happened to him.

You be the judge.

Title: *The Rescue of Vincent*

- Author: Bob Doerr
- Publisher: TotalRecall Publications, Inc.
- Paper Back: ISBN: 978-1-59095-279-5
- eBook: ISBN: 978-1-59095-280-1
- Audio ISBN: 978-1-59095-281-8
- Number of pages in the finished book: 130
- Publication Date: : October 28, 2015

Would you believe in the magic of a coin you discover that has your name inscribed on it? The coin claims to be magical and even has instructions for you to follow. Would you follow them? What if you did? Would you expect anything to happen?

That's what happened to Ricky Street. He found the coin and followed its instructions. What happened to him was totally unexpected and quite frightening. It led him to an adventure that many might think impossible to believe, but it did.

You be the judge.

Title: *The Magic of Vix*

- Author: Bob Doerr
- Publisher: TotalRecall Publications, Inc.
- Paper Back: ISBN: 978-1-59095-309-9
- eBook: ISBN: 978-1-59095-280-1
- Audio ISBN: 978-1-59095-281-8
- Number of pages in the finished book: 140
- Publication Date: August 4, 2015

Samantha Gillespie's discovery of a magic coin results in her transportation to the strange world of Vex where magic is real and where she has to overcome a number of challenges if she ever hopes to return home.

What happened to Samantha was totally unexpected and quite frightening. It led her to an adventure that many might think impossible to believe, but it did.

You be the judge.

For a complete list of books by Bob Doerr,
a preview of upcoming titles and more
visit his website www.bobdoerr.com or
find him on Facebook.

Titles by Bob Doerr

Mystery Detective Suspense Thrillers

Dead Men Can Kill

Cold Winters Kill

Another Colorado Kill

Loose Ends Kill

No One Else To Kill

Caffeine Can Kill

-Greed Can Kill

Action Adventure Series

The Attack

The Group

The Assassins

For a complete list of books by Bob Doerr,
a previews of upcoming titles, a schedule of events
and more visit his website www.bobdoerr.com or
find him on Facebook.

A Mouse Gate Adventure Book
What's your adventure?
www.mousegate.com